Hezekiah Butterworth, H. Winthrop Peirce

The Patriot Schoolmaster

The adventures of the two Boston cannon, the ''Adams'' and ''Hancock''

Hezekiah Butterworth, H. Winthrop Peirce

The Patriot Schoolmaster
The adventures of the two Boston cannon, the "Adams" and "Hancock"

ISBN/EAN: 9783337088439

Printed in Europe, USA, Canada, Australia, Japan

Cover: Foto ©Andreas Hilbeck / pixelio.de

More available books at **www.hansebooks.com**

Allie in the British camp.

THE
PATRIOT SCHOOLMASTER

OR, THE ADVENTURES OF THE TWO BOSTON CANNON, THE "ADAMS" AND "HANCOCK"

A Tale of the Minute Men and the Sons of Liberty

BY

HEZEKIAH BUTTERWORTH

AUTHOR OF THE BOYS OF GREENWAY COURT, IN THE BOYHOOD OF LINCOLN,
THE LOG SCHOOL-HOUSE ON THE COLUMBIA, ZIGZAG JOURNEYS,
STORY OF THE HYMNS, ETC.

ILLUSTRATED BY H. WINTHROP PEIRCE

NEW YORK
D. APPLETON AND COMPANY
1896

PREFACE.

THIS volume relates to Sam Adams, the leader of
the Boston town-meeting, who was called in his
day "The Father of America," one of the most
lovable men in our history. The story follows the events
associated with the two guns the "Adams" and "Hancock,"
or the "Hancock" and "Adams," which were hidden from
the British forces by a patriot schoolmaster and his equally
patriotic schoolboys, in several mysterious ways, until they
could be taken into the American lines. These small cannon, which were once the pride of the Ancient and Honorable Artillery, may now be seen in the chamber at the
top of Bunker Hill Monument, where the reader may visit
them.

The volume completes four stories of the four most
unselfish and patriotic leaders in American progress: Sam
Adams, George Washington, Abraham Lincoln, and Mar-
cus Whitman, the latter the Pacific pioneer. The three
volumes last named have been very generously received
by the public, and the writer will be more than pleased if
the story of noble old Sam Adams shall have as kindly a

reception. Ruskin makes the desire to praise some noble
character or thing the first principle of inspiration, and one
must have a slow heart who would not feel such an inspiration to write of the hero of the town-meeting in the old
Boston days.

The writer has lived among the historic associations of
many of the events and traditions herein described for
some twenty years, and has loved to visit the places which
he here attempts to picture. The story is an historical
fiction, and he has taken the liberties allowed to this class
of writing; but nearly all of the incidents, except such as
are essential to the movement of a story, have a basis of
truth or well-ordered tradition, and in this manner he has
sought to give a picture of old Boston in its heroic days.
The reader will not find it hard to trace in the monuments
and historical places of Boston the principal scenes of the
story, if he be interested to do so. The two cannon;
Faneuil Hall; the Old South Church; the Granary Burying-ground, where Adams, Hancock, Crispus Attucks, and
so many of the patriots sleep; the statue of Adams; the
portraits of Hancock, and the many pictures of the
Hancock house; the Common; Dorchester Heights; the
grounds and monument at Bunker Hill—all pass before
the eye of the lover of history, who looks to see the sem-
blance of old associations amid new scenes. New Boston
contains the old, and has well marked its historic places.
If this volume shall help any one better to read the heroic

spirit of the past, it will serve the purpose for which it was written. Even Queue was a real dog, and Phillis Wheatley a real person; and characters corresponding to Dr. Oliver were well known. The writer has simply followed, for the most part, the facts, incidents, and traditions associated with the two guns.

Of Samuel Adams himself the picture is not overdrawn, and it is a pleasure to write of such an heroic character. Wells, in his great biography of Adams, says of him, in summing up his life:

"No blandishments of flattery could lull his vigilance, no sophistry deceive his penetration. Difficulties could not discourage his decision, nor danger appall his fortitude. He had also an affable and persuasive address, which could reconcile conflicting interests and promote harmony in action. He never, from jealousy, checked the advancement of others; and, in accomplishing great deeds, he took to himself no praise. Seeking fame as little as fortune, and office less than either, he aimed steadily at the good of his country and the best interests of mankind. Of despondency he knew nothing; trials only nerved him for severer struggles; his sublime and unfaltering hope had a cast of solemnity, and was as much a part of his nature as if his confidence sprang from an insight into divine decrees. For himself and for others, he held that all sorrows and losses were to be encouraged rather than that liberty should perish."

H. B.

CONTENTS.

vii

viii

LIST OF ILLUSTRATIONS.

CHAPTER I.

LE Surry am done made a discobery!" So said a sharp-eyed colored woman to Mary Fayreweather. "An' your own boys was in it!"

Mary Fayreweather was a widow, and had three sons. The two older sons were named Andrew and Philip, and were companions, and their attachment to each other was often remarked in Boston town. They were young men. The youngest son was named Albert—"little Allie" he was called. He was now about twelve years of age.

These were stirring times in old Boston town: the Revolution was near at hand, and perhaps the most excited soul at this eventful period was Old Surry, "a slave woman," as she was called, belonging to the wife of Samuel Adams. "A *slave* woman belonging to the family of the patriot Samuel Adams!" the reader will exclaim. Yes. She was a gift to Mrs. Adams, and when Sam Adams one day said to her, "Surry, I'll set you free; this is to be a land of freedom," or like

words, the old woman almost went into convulsions.
The manner in which she expressed her indignation was
an old-time Boston story.

"Free from yo', Massa Adams! free from yo'! Ole
Surry might as well be free from de good Lord. I
always was free *wid* yo', Massa Adams. Don't Ole
Surry have her own head? Free! I'd cry my eyes
out, Ole Surry would, now. Wot was dat story about
Ruth yo' read in de family last night, Massa Adams?
'Entreat me not to leabe thee.' I'll neber leabe yo',
Massa Adams: in my eyes yo' be a bigger man den de
king wid all his lions and unicorns. Lor', Massa Adams,
wot do chilern all do? Don't de chilern all follow yo' in
de streets, Massa Adams? Do yo' think Ole Surry's
eber goin' to leabe a man like dat? Oh, Massa Adams,
Massa Adams!"

Old Surry buried her face in her white apron, and
rocked to and fro in great agitation.

"I did not want you to go away, Surry, but I must do
what is right; the man of the town meeting, you know,
must do just what is right. I only wanted to say that
you were free to be free if you wished to be free. That
is just right, isn't it, Old Surry?" •

"Massa Adams, 'fore de Lord, dat am jest right."

"There's no more faithful heart in my family than
yours, Surry, only you are a little too curious sometimes
—a *little* too curious about public things, Surry."

"Dat am so, Massa Adams; and, Massa Adams, Ole Surry am done made a discobery."

Sam Adams suspected that. He slowly moved away, followed by his remarkable dog, Queue, which became a terror to every redcoat who found himself alone in an out-of-the-way place near the Adams house at a period a little later in our history. The words, "Ole Surry am done made a discobery," were often repeated by the dark-faced woman during the exciting scenes which led to the war.

Old Surry, being Mrs. Adams's maid, had unusual social privileges; among them was that of calling upon her neighbors; and as her master was the man of public affairs, and as she had a very inquisitive mind, she was very welcome to the white families.

The Widow Fayreweather lived just across the way from the Adams house and gardens, which overlooked the harbor and the sea. Old Surry delighted to cross the street and go neighboring to the Fayreweathers'. Little Allie Fayreweather was a favorite of Sam Adams; the boy adopted, as it were, the patriot as his father, and he came to be known as "Sam Adams's boy." He had been given a small drum, and he often followed the patriot with it, drumming.

The town meeting man's dog was at his heels most of the time, and "Little Allie" much of the time, the latter with his drum.

Old Surry was very superstitious. She feared the red-

2

coats much, but "hants," as she termed the supposed
beings called ghosts, more. As much as she was afraid
of seeing "hants," she was always looking for them; and
the evening before the opening of this tale, she had crept
up what is now West and Wasnington Streets to the gun-
house, at the front of the Common. She hardly knew
why she went there; it was probably on account of the
superstition in her nature. She used to go out nights and
wander around the hearse-house at a distance. The gun-
house, like the hearse-house, interested her. She had
visions of battles there—of such battles as she may have
heard Sam Adams read about in the Bible and Josephus's
" History of the Jewish Wars."

The writing-school house, where Master Holbrooke, the
patriot, taught (not Master Holbrooke, the Tory), stood at
the front of the Common next to the gun-house. While
Old Surry was surveying the gun-house in awe under the
moon and stars, the wind from the harbor breathing mysteriously through the great elms, and scattering the September leaves down to the streets, she heard low voices
in the schoolhouse. But the schoolhouse was dark. Old
Surry's curiosity was even stronger than her fear of the
mysterious beings which she called " hants." She crept
by the gun-house, and sat down on the turf at the back
of the schoolhouse to listen. She heard voices:

" Four guns——— "

" Wood-box——— "

" Coal——— "

" Blacksmith's shop———"

" Promise secrecy———"

" Can hurt you, boys——— "

Whose voice was tha' which spoke last? It was certainly Master Holbrooke's, the patriot schoolmaster. And in two of the other voices Old Surry recognized Andrew and Philip Fayreweather.

" I'll never tell."

Whose voice was that?

It was little Allie's—" Sam Adams's boy."

Old Surry rose up. She would have confidences with the Widow Fayreweather now.

She hurried home, saying: " Signs and wonders! signs and wonders! But wot need Ole Surry mind—don't Sam Adams hold America in his two fists? Dat's wot he does, now!"

The moon hung over the sea and the Castle as Old Surry shut the gate and stole into her home under the fruit-trees of the garden. The great vane over the Province House was turning to and fro, and as the poor slave woman marked it she said, " Dar am comin' a storm," and so there was, in another sense. There were sentinels pacing to and fro in Boston town.

Old Surry did not sleep much that night. The next morning she early went across the street to the Widow Fayreweather's, with the mysterious words with which

this chapter begins, "Ole Surry am done made a discobery, an' your own boys was in it!"

"I will look into this matter," said the widow.   "I
shall be sharp; but honor flows in the blood of my three
boys.   I believe in my boys, and they believe in me.   It
is the times which makes these mysteries."

"Mis' Fayreweather, dat am so.   But Ole Surry can
see double.   Allie, yo' know, am a drummer—natural
like.   Mis' Fayreweather, wot do I tink?   When I see
him go 'long the street, rub-a-dub, after Massa Adams—
rub-a-dub, rub-a-dub—I jest tink dat he is preparin':
to wot, I don't know; but preparin', Mis' Fayreweather.
Dat boy'll drum again some day.   I don't know whar',
but he will.   You'll tink some day o' wot Ole Surry
say!"

CHAPTER II.

LLIE FAYREWEATHER, come here. Sit down there, and be sober now. Did Master Holbrooke ever give you a whipping at school?"

"Of course he did, mother: you don't think that I'm dull, do you? Why, ain't I as smart as other boys?"

"Ay, Allie Fayreweather, you are as smart as other boys, and smarter, too, than some, I reckon. But that isn't neither here nor there. When did he whip you *last?*"

"Last year."

"He has not whipped you this year?"

"No, not that I remember, mother."

"I thought not, and you would have been most likely to have remembered it if he had. Boys recollect Master Holbrooke's whippings. He is not sparing in such benefits. Why has he not corrected you this year, Allie? Are you not as smart as you used to be?"

"Not that way, mother."

"Allie, my boy, you and the schoolmaster have been

7

getting very intimate of late—been putting your two
heads together after school. And Snyder, that poor German boy, he seems to be in the schoolmaster's confidence,
too. What are you plotting? What makes you go around
with your thoughts in the air, wool-gathering, forgetful-
like? I never saw a boy so absent-minded as you have
become. I would think that you were going daft. I
have to charge you over and over to do a thing, or you
forget it. When I asked you only yesterday to go to the
store to get some pepper and salt, and not to bring back
anything else, you ran off at break-neck speed, saying,
' Pepper and salt, pepper and salt!' and then tumbled heels
over head, and got up and ran on, exclaiming, ' Powder
and shot, powder and shot!' What is your mind running
on such things as those for? What have you to do with
powder and shot?"

"These are stirring times, mother. General Gage's
troops are on their way here—have you not heard?"

" Coming to protect the colonies?"

" No, not to protect them, Mr. Adams thinks."

" What, then?"

" To enslave them. He shall never enslave *me!* "

" Tut, tut, hear that now! Anybody would think that
you were a whole army, you and Snyder and Master Holbrooke. I guess that you have forgotten that the gun-
house and four cannon in it, too, stand next door to the
schoolhouse, and one clap of one of those cannon would

set you all flying in like a windmill. When you get up
your rebellion, take with you a flag of truce—you will
surely need it. What notions Master Holbrooke is putting
into the heads of his boys! When General Gage takes
possession of those cannon, there'll be a still school."

"Mother, that will never be."

"What—what will never be?"

"The day when General Gage gets hold of those four
cannon in the gun-house."

"Allie, do I hear my ears? What's goin' to prevent
him, I'd like to know? The writin'-school on the Common? General Gage will be the military commander of
the colony, of course he will; and you don't suppose that
he will let those four cannon, sent over for the protection
of the colony, remain without a guard! You'll find a
guard at the next door to the schoolhouse some day."

"And what if when the guard arrives he shall find
nothing in the gun-house?"

"No cannon there?"

"Yes."

"He'd hang the schoolmaster, perhaps, and all the
school. There's trees enough on the Common."

"I think not, mother."

"Why?"

"O mother, you are bantering me! Ask my brothers,
mother."

"But why your brothers, Allie?"

"They were *there.*"

"There?"

The boy was silent.

"Where?"

The boy did not answer.

"A boy should be at no place where he would be un-willing that his mother should see him."

"Yes, but Mr. Adams knows, and Master Holbrooke. They would not encourage me to do any wrong thing. But why do you not ask my older brothers about this thing?"

"They were *there?*"

"Yes."

The Widow Fayreweather arose, and walked the room.

"Allie?"

"Well, mother?"

"I shall never ask Andrew and Philip about this strange matter. My two boys have always done just right, and they have one heart. I can trust them, and ask no ques-tions. Heaven be praised for sons like those! Yet I would spare them to the cause—yes, I would spare them to the cause. I know what Mr. Adams thinks—that the colonies ought to resist the British power, and become a nation of themselves, governed after the manner of the folkmote."

"Mother, you trust Andrew and Philip, why do you not me?"

" You are younger, Allie."

" Would you give me to the cause? "

" You—my own little Allie? Let me ask my heart—
let me ask my God. Yes, I would give my all to the
cause of liberty. What is life worth but to obey the in-
ward voice, and make better all humankind? "

" Who has told you something, mother? "

" Oh, never mind, Allie. Come here, and let us read
together the Psalm."

As they were reading there was heard a boom of cannon
on the sea. Mrs. Fayreweather listened. She arose, and,
followed by Allie, opened the door.

Sam Adams stood on the sidewalk before his house,
listening, and looking at the puffs of smoke that were rising silvery and gray into the air of the sea and harbor.

" Mr. Adams," said the widow, " what does that mean? "

" War, perhaps."

" If it comes, what will be done with the four cannon
next to the schoolhouse? "

" I've been thinking over those things, madam. I don't
know. We must let events shape themselves. But those
cannon must never be turned against us—never!"

" And they never shall be," said little Allie Fayreweather.

" Do you hear that, Mr. Adams? Allie has been so
much in your company that he talks more like a man
than a boy."

Old Surry came out, her head bobbing.   She had heard
Allie, and added:

"De young rooster has crowed, and now dere's no
more need to be said.   Dat boy will fight de king some
day.   It's comin'—war, war, war—I kin feel it in my
bones."

Sam Adams passed on with a smile that shaded into a
serious line of thought.   Just then there was a booming
of guns at the Castle.   The troops ordered by General
Gage, who was the captain-general of all the British forces
in North America, with headquarters at that time in New
York, were coming into the harbor from Halifax.

It was Saturday, September 27, 1768—a dazzling day,
with the still bright lustres that cover the New England
hills in the time of the coloring of leaves and of the
golden-rod.

Boom!   Boom!

Sam Adams turned and looked out on the still blue sea.
In him was embodied the spirit of America.   On that day
he was, as it were, America.   The people of Boston had
resolved to resist the landing of the British troops in the
town.

Boom!   Boom!

The troops sent to coerce the freemen of the town
meetings were at hand.   Would they be left at the Castle?

Bells began to ring; people were hurrying to and fro.
Sam Adams saw the red cross of England lifting over

the blue sea, and the first smoke of the long Revolutionary contest rising into the air. He was about to hurry away to join the citizens on the wharves, when he was courteously accosted by his little friend, Allie Fayreweather.

"Mr. Adams," said Allie, lifting his hat, "will the citizens not seize the cannon in the gun-house right away for their own safety?"

"That would be a declaration of war. They must obey the governor's orders until the crisis comes—unless—well, you know."

"Mr. Adams, pardon me, but will not the town regiments want them right away for their own use?"

"I hope not, my boy, but I think that they will in time."

"Mr. Adams, what would happen *if* those cannon should disappear?"

The hero of the town meeting looked puzzled. He lifted his hands, and gazed at the boy full in the face in silence.

Boom!

Sam Adams, without making any answer to the question, turned away and joined the excited people on the wharves.

How the people peered out on the blue harbor on that bright September day! Boston then was a three-hilled town. The Province House, with the English flag flying in the air and its vane of the Golden Indian, rose over the houses near the spire of the Old South Church. The hills around the harbor were covered with oaks and savins. In the middle of the harbor rose the Castle, now Fort Independence, with the British flag flying. The sky was serene and cloudless, and the air had the hollow stillness peculiar to September days.

Allie with his drum had followed Sam Adams down to the wharves. As the British were landing, there came wafted across the harbor some sprightly music from their regimental band. It was so enlivening that it well-nigh set the excited people to dancing. It was probably the first time that the tune to become historically famous as "Yankee Doodle" was heard in Boston.

"Rub-a-dub-dub, dub-dub-dub," said Allie. "I'd like to catch that tune. I wish that they would play it again. Let us go over to Dorchester Hill to listen."

Sam Adams yielded to the gentle persuasion. Dorchester Heights, or Hill, as it was then, looked down upon the town and the Castle. A long bridge, near which is the Farragut statue, now connects South Boston with Fort Independence, where the Castle stood. The Heights is now an historic park, with cool trees, seats, a monumental inscription, and a flag-staff. It was in this neighborhood that the Pilgrims of the "Mary and John," or the first settlers of Dorchester, probably held their first Thanksgiving.

It was now near night. Sam Adams hurried toward

Boston Neck, absent in thought, followed by Allie, who from time to time tried the new tune on his drum :

Rub-a-dub-dub, rub-a-dub.

" I could play that tune if I could hear it once more," said Allie.

" Perhaps they will play it again," said Mr. Adams.

It was sunset when they reached the Heights. Looking down on the glimmering harbor, in the direction of where the Perkins Institute for the Blind now stands, the Castle and the newly arrived ships lay clear in the still mellow light.

The troops were drawn up before the Castle, and hark ! The band began to play : the same tune as before. It seemed to make the very hills merry. It was the old English air of " Nancy Dawson " or " Lucy Locket," which it is now claimed may have been used in derision of the soldiers of Cromwell. A surgeon of the British Army at Albany, in 1755, wrote a song, and sang it to the same air in ridicule of the New England troops, who, in the war of that date, presented a very uncouth appearance, being uniformed much like the Ancient and Honorable Artillery in their annual parades of to-day, each soldier wearing his own dress. The historians tell us that after the landing of the British troops at Castle William, then the Castle, "this tune was the capital piece of the Band of Music." The song in derision of Washington's troops, set to this tune, was written in 1775. It begins :

"Father and I went down to camp,
        Along with Captain Goodwin,
    Where we *see* the men and boys,
        As thick as hasty-puddin'.

"There was *Captain* Washington,
        Upon a slapping stallion,
    A-giving orders to the men,
        I *guess* there was a million."

The air was played at the surrender of Burgoyne, and much at the close of the Revolution. We shall return to this story again.

Allie listened to the lively tune with intense interest. He began to drum:

"Rub-a-dub-dub, rub-a-dub,
        Rub-a-dub-dub-dub-dub;
    Rub-a-dub-dub, rub-a-dub,
        Rub-a-dub-dub-dub-dub."

"I've caught it!" said the boy. He listened. The band at the Castle were playing it over again. He followed the band on his own little drum.

"It means war," said Sam Adams, shaking his head. The moon was rising over the sea; there was a coolness in the air. He paced to and fro. "It means war—war!"

"Mr. Adams, I can drum."

"We may all have to follow the drum, Allie. Let's go."

"Mr. Adams, I can drum that tune, and I will."

They went down toward the Neck. Sam Adams was silent, but Allie followed him, drumming that tune over and over, and thus they came to the lights of their neighboring homes.

The next day was Sunday. To the horror of all, news came to the customary worshippers in the Old North and in the Old South Church (as that church is now called) that the ships which had been moored near the Castle were approaching the wharves. The people gathered again and gazed out on the sea. Were the regiments ordered here by General Gage coming to enslave them? Was this the beginning of a war with an uncertain end?

It was Sunday, and the ships neared the wharves and unloaded a part of the troops, under the cover of the guns. The British soldiers landed with charged muskets, fixed bayonets, and drums beating. They marched to the Common, and planted the cannon before the Town House. It was only a question now as to which should be the future ruler of America, Sam Adams, as representing the people in town-meeting, or George III.; whether the king should suppress Sam Adams, who represented the spirit of American liberty, or whether Sam Adams should discrown the king in these American colonies. It was Sam Adams's purpose, at this period, to build up a new and independent nation; it was the purpose of most of the other patriots simply to secure their charter rights under the king.

CHAPTER III.

LLIE, if you trust a boy he can keep a secret. We make folks true by believing them. If a man had but one good quality, the chances are if you were to praise it, it would grow and root out his evils. I do not use the rod as much as I did, as you may have noticed; I believe in men more than I did—and in boys.

" Allie, there are serious times at hand. I can feel it coming, just as Old Surry says that she can feel events coming ' in her bones.' "

" Is it war? " asked Allie.

" Sam Adams says it is war."

" For what, Master Holbrooke ? "

" For human rights; there is a principle at stake."

" But it would not hurt us to drink taxed tea," said Allie. " Parson Byles says that the crown has taken off the taxes from all other goods."

" Yes, but the principle is the same. Lord North's bill has repealed all the duties laid on the colonies except tea. That is well; but don't you see, Allie, that by keeping up the tax on tea he maintains the right of the crown to tax the colonies? The young women of the town are forming a society to pledge themselves to drink no more taxed tea. Allie, we must form such a society in the school. I must make my boys patriots—patriots—patriots, Allie, and I will. A master is his school. All that I am, I am ready to offer to my country, and my boys must have the same mind."

The above dialogue took place in Sam Adams's garden, and Old Surry heard it with uplifted hands, saying now and then: "For de land's sake, de times of signs and wonders am comin'!"

Late in the evening Master Holbrooke and Allie Fayreweather turned away from Sam Adams's garden. The September moon had risen high, like a night sun. The ships in the harbor twinkled in the blue distance under the high lights of the Castle, on one side, and on the other side of the water lay the hills in cool, still shadows.

"There is something awful in the stillness of this night," said Master Holbrooke, "and I wish to talk out of the hearing of Old Surry's ears. The negro woman is watching us, but her heart is loyal. Allie, you will one day see blood flow in the streets of Boston. It belongs to me to teach my school patriotism. My place is with my boys."

"Will the troops take possession of the cannon in the gun-house, do you suppose?"

3

" I have told you and the boys, privately, that no regiments that are here to oppress us must ever be allowed
to turn those cannon against the people."

" You said that if the troops came, the guns must be
hidden.   Where? "

" Walk slowly, my boy.   I must think over the matter.
How would it do to form a private company among the
boys in the school to watch and protect the cannon?
Nearly all the boys are sons of the ' Sons of Liberty.' "

" But, Master Holbrooke, what if a single boy were to
prove false, and tell, and the plan were to come to the
ears of the governor? "

" There is not one false-hearted boy in the school.   I
know men, and I know boys.   I shall trust in you as a
leader, and poor little Snyder might act as a messenger
for us.   He is light and nimble, with a heart true as steel.
No one would suspect him."

" How would it do, Master Holbrooke, to form in the
school a guard for the gun-house? "

" It should be a secret society, and should bring into it
the old members of the school."

" What should the secret be? "

" This, Allie : that if any movement should be made by
the troops to take away the cannon to use against the
people, we will hide them, or at least act as a watch for
the Sons of Liberty.   I have thought of that.   We will
form a secret society in the school to watch the guns.

Others have their own duties: it is my duty to make patriots of my own school."

" But the troops might seize them without warning."

" No, the guns belong to our own citizens, and they would not be taken away by the troops before there were open hostilities of some kind. The Sons of Liberty would know of the coming danger."

" But where could we hide them?"

" I will call a secret meeting of the boys to-morrow evening in the schoolroom. We will then talk over the taxed tea and all these plans."

The two parted under the old elm, and the high tide on the marshes around the Common glimmered in the moonlight. The great tree, which had been used for a place of execution in witchcraft days, was dropping its first leaves at the foot of the hill near the pond. Young Master Holbrooke turned away in one direction and Allie Fayreweather in another. The patriot schoolmaster had perfect confidence in the heart of the little boy.

Andrew and Philip Fayreweather had been pupils of the writing-school. The next day Master Holbrooke went to them, and said:

" You write well, but you need more education."

The young men understood him.

Said Andrew, " We will enter your *evening* classes."

" And we will have an evening class to-night; not a secret one."

It was a large evening class of manly boys that assembled that night. Some of them had met at the night
meetings there, such as Old Surry had overheard, when
Master Holbrooke had talked in the dark and hinted at
the danger of war, and that in that case the school should
watch the guns in the gun-house. He had now something to say to all in the open school, and afterward he
would continue the secret part of his plan with a few boys
whom he knew he could best trust.

"My boys," said the patriot schoolmaster, "I am going
to talk with you directly and plainly. You know that I
believe that the crown has no right to tax the colonies
without their consent. How many of you think as I do?
Let those who think so raise their right hands."

Every right hand was raised.

"My boys, if a thing is right, it is right, and there need
no more be said about it. If a thing is wrong, it is wrong,
and there need no more be said about that. If England
has the right to tax one thing, she has the right to tax
many things. Tea is a luxury; but if the crown has a
right to tax the tea sent to the colonies, it has a right to
tax all goods sent to the colonies.

"The daughters of the Sons of Liberty have just formed
a society. I want you to hear the resolution that they
have adopted. Listen:

"'We, the daughters of those patriots who have and
do now appear for the public interest, and in that prin-

cipally regard their posterity, as such do with pleasure engage with them in denying ourselves the drinking of foreign tea, in hope to frustrate a plan which tends to deprive a whole community of all that is valuable in life.'

" Do you hear that, boys? ' We, the daughters of the patriots.' How many of you are willing to subscribe to this resolution: ' We, the boys of the Common writing-school, will never use any article that is taxed by the English crown without the consent of the colonies '? 'As many as are willing to write your names to that, stand up."

Every boy arose.

" That is all for the present. You may take your copy-books."

The nine-o'clock bells rang.

" You are now dismissed."

A part of the boys went out into the street, but there were seven who remained in the schoolroom, and these, an hour later, were gathered around a single dim light. Three of the seven were the Fayreweather brothers, and one was the little German boy, Allie's friend, Snyder. The other three boys were of like positive character. The ages of the seven boys ranged from eleven or twelve to seventeen, except Andrew Fayreweather, who was older.

The room grew very still.

" Boys," said the master, " we have agreed not to use taxed goods. That is well. But there is another duty

that falls to us—I feel it does; we have talked of it
already. The four cannon in the gun-house belong to the
citizens of Boston; they are the *only* field-cannon that belong to the citizens of Boston; the batteries belong to the
crown. They are likely to be the only cannon that will
belong to the citizens of Boston for a long time. The
Sons of Liberty must always control them. They are
housed here in the very school-grounds. We must have
an eye upon them. This matter that we have talked
over in our dark meetings assumes a greater importance
now. You are seven boys who can be trusted. I must
make a guard of you."

"What shall we be called?" asked little Snyder.

"You might be called a little Son of Liberty," said
Master Holbrooke, "you or Allie; but that term would
not apply to the rest. Suppose I call you 'The Younger
Sons of Liberty,' although Andrew Fayreweather is one
of the Sons of Liberty."

"'The Younger Sons of Liberty,'" replied Andrew
Fayreweather; "and our purpose shall be to guard the
guns in the gun-house and prevent their falling into the
hands of any enemy of the people of Boston."

"Exactly," said the schoolmaster; "you have expressed
yourself well."

"Master Holbrooke," said Andrew, "if it ever became
necessary to conceal those guns, how could it best be
done?"

"Well said again, Andrew; but seven are too many to discuss such a question."

"A wood-bin would be a good place," said Snyder.

"A coal-bin would be a better one," said Allie.

"A load of kelp would be better still," said little Snyder.

Master Holbrooke smiled at the suggestions of the two little boys. Then Philip Fayreweather spoke :

"I think, Master Holbrooke, that as you have said seven is too large a number to be intrusted with any such secret as this, there ought to be no more in the secret than would be able to move the heaviest of those cannon."

"You are right, Andrew," said Master Holbrooke; "there should not be more than four in the secret. We must have a secret committee."

"That puts me out," said little Snyder.

"And me," said Allie.

"Yes," said Master Holbrooke; "you can lift some, but you would hardly be equal to the task of one of those cannon. Who shall be the secret committee?"

"I would nominate you, Master Holbrooke, and Big Ben Adams, and my two big brothers," said Allie.

"A very magnanimous thought for a little boy like you, Allie. Do you second the motion, Snyder?"

"Yes, yes."

"Do you all approve?"

All approved.

The town clock struck ten.

"What is the first thing for us to do?" asked Andrew Fayreweather.

"To go over to the gun-house and see if we can handle the guns in an emergency. We will do that now"

The master took a lantern and led the way. He knew how to effect an entrance to the gun-house, and the committee were soon experimenting and making trials of their strength.

"Boys," said Master Holbrooke, "let us make those guns our trust."

"And pledge our honor to defend them," said Andrew Fayreweather.

"And to stand or fall by them," said Allie, with a resolution larger than his slight form.

"You?" said Master Holbrooke.

"Yes," said Allie. "I can drum, and if needs be, I can fall by them, as well as my brothers."

"Stand in a class, boys. How many will pledge your honor to these guns?"

Every boy lifted his hand in the shadows.

"Well done. I will pledge all that I have to the cause of American liberty."

"And where will we be ten years from now?" asked Philip Fayreweather.

"You laugh at me," said Allie, "because I am small. But you have let me into your secret, and I also know what Mr. Adams thinks is likely to come. I will make my pledge as good as any; wait and see. I have learned a new tune, which makes one step lively."

" You speak well, Allie," said Master Holbrooke. " We may have occasion to recall this night again."

They moved about in the shadows, and Allie threw himself upon one of the guns and rested upon it, while the master was talking in low tones to Andrew and Philip.

They were so interested as to almost forget the outer world, when suddenly there came a voice, as it were out of the air:

" Wot yo' doin'?"

They heard a patter on the grass, and seemed to see a fleeing form among the shadows of the vague objects of the night.

The secret committee walked out on the Common, and sat down under the old elm by the glassy pond. The night was still. A sentinel was pacing to and fro in the distance, and here and there was a solitary light.

" Do you know," said Master Holbrooke, " I am thinking that those two little boys, Snyder and Allie, suggested some bright things in case of an emergency. Cannon covered with wood, coal, or kelp would not excite suspicion. Cover the guns with sticks of wood, and put them into a great wood-bin, and who would know but that they were logs; or in a charcoal-bin, who would know but that they were unbroken coal?"

"But how could that be done?" asked Andrew Fayre-weather.

"Well, we have a large oak wood-box in the school-room; and Blingo—he is a blacksmith."

"I move that we add Blingo to our secret committee," said Andrew.

Every one saw the point and approved it.

"Blingo has a kelp-cart," said Andrew. "He could remove the guns to his blacksmith shop in the night, and when they were once buried in his coal-bin, who would find them?"

The secret committee sat long under the old elm, and discussed these matters. The patriot schoolmaster saw the future, but not the seasons of the crises; it would be a long time yet before these four guns would be needed to defend the liberties that were now threatened.

A watchman came around, and warned the master that he and his boys were keeping late hours.

The boys of Master Holbrooke's school, a hundred or more in number, were from this time schooled in patriot-ism. And the patriotism was a new one; it was in touch with Sam Adams's idea that the colonies should form a new nation, and be governed on the old town-meeting principle that he had himself established in the town of Boston at Faneuil Hall—a nation whose governing power should be the sense of the majority of the people as ex-pressed in intelligent discussion followed by honest votes.

The capitol of this nation should be another Faneuil Hall,
and the people should govern the whole by elected representatives. The presiding officer, or president, should be
but another Samuel Adams. The compact on board the
" Mayflower" first embodied this idea; then the New
England town-meeting, or folkmote, which found its most
conspicuous example in the Boston town-meeting, over
which Sam Adams was usually elected president. In
that town-meeting Sam Adams beheld the model of a
new nation; he in reality was the prophet of the republic;
and like Moses, who saw the pattern of the tabernacle in
the mount, and was commanded to make all things after
the pattern shown to him on the mount, he had a vision
of the whole fabric of government which is to-day the
United States.

Sam Adams rests in the Granary Burying-ground, and,
like Hancock's, his grave is almost unmarked. At the
present writing a peanut-stand stands near it. Where are
ye, O Sons of the Revolution? A nation is known by
the character of the men they crown, and here is work to
do which would honor you.

Other patriots received honors and money, but Sam
Adams seems hardly to have thought of such things; he
worked for a cause. His happiness was in his dreams of
the future, when America should be free, and her ruling
power should be her own voice. Glorious old Sam
Adams! Remove the peanut-stand, and set a monument

in the sun where his remains rest in the graveyard of
Hancock and the family of Franklin, and those who fell
in the Boston massacre.

And make there a monument to Hancock, who is said
to have kept poor Adams from going to jail for debt, and
to the wife of Hancock, who fled with her child at her
breast to follow the fortunes of her exiled husband!

O precious plots of the old Granary Burying-ground,
did ever an abbey hold such worth! The seasons come
and go, and the bright, happy faces pass by the cool trees
over the graves between the Park Street Church and the
Tremont House in endless procession, but the old Puritan
graves grow hollow, and the simple memorial stones sink
down into them. The place may one day be a congress
of monuments, a garden of the illustrious dead.

But if Sam Adams has no monument here, his bronze
form stands in the Square, in view of Faneuil Hall. One
may read there that he was "fearless and incorruptible,"
a "leader of the people," and that he "organized the
Revolution." It makes one taller to pass that strong face
as it reviews for all time the busy multitudes.

CHAPTER IV.

SOME STRANGE BUT REAL PEOPLE.

NNIE!" called Mrs. Fayreweather. A beautiful girl of some twenty summers entered the open door of the Widow Fayreweather's house. Her name was Annie Moore. She was some day to be the bride of Andrew Fayreweather, and the whole family loved her.

"Why do you call my name in such a sad tone, *mother?*" said the girl. Andrew had asked her to call his mother "mother," though her wedding-day might not yet be appointed.

"Annie, I fear that there are sorry times at hand. If the colonies should resist the crown, you know what my two boys might do—and who can tell what their fate would be?"

": Don't you worry, Annie," said Philip; "if any one in this family has to bear arms, it will be I. I am not engaged to wed. Andrew is, and I am glad it is to you, Annie. I was glad when he told me he loved you, and for your sake, Annie, if war comes, it will be I that will

go.   Andrew has been a true brother to me, as he will
be a true husband to you, and I would protect him with
my life."

"And I will go too, Annie," said Allie.   "If Mr. Adams
goes, I shall go."

"But what could you do, my boy?" asked Mrs. Fayreweather.

"I can drum, and I can carry messages."

It was a mild October night.   The trees were coloring,
and the sails lay white in the harbor.   People were gathering on the corners of the streets and in shops, all of
them talking about the arrival of the troops, and of the
injustice of the placing of the town under military rule.

Old Surry was hanging lanterns about Sam Adams's
garden, and one by one the neighbors gathered there
under the trees.   They felt that Faneuil Hall, the place of
the town-meeting, and not the Province House, was the
real seat of power in Boston now, and that somehow Sam
Adams's word would determine future events.   Every
one wished to know what he thought and what he might
say.

John Hancock, in courtly dress, came down to the garden early in the evening.   Sam Adams was poor; Hancock was rich, but Hancock was always glad to share his
wealth with Adams.   The latter had declared his own
independence when, in 1743, on receiving the degree of
Master of Arts he read a thesis on the subject, "Whether

it be Lawful to Resist the Supreme Magistrate, if the Commonwealth cannot otherwise be Preserved." Governor Shirley and the officials of the crown sat near him when he read the thesis, and were alarmed to hear him announce the duty of resistance to oppression. He began to work secretly for the cause of the independence of the colonies in 1765, and to avow himself a revolutionist in 1769.

Among the visitors on this evening was queer old Mather Byles, of Hollis Street Church, the wit of the town. He was a stanch royalist.

Holbrooke, the patriot schoolmaster, was there, and his boys came flocking after him. He had once been a severe disciplinarian, and his school had stood in awe of him, but his boys had come to be remarkably fond of him of late. It was suspected in all the town that they shared some secret in common, but what it was no one out of the circle seemed to know, unless it was Blingo, the leather-aproned blacksmith, whose shop was at the North End. It was reported that the master and his boys held meetings in the dark in the schoolhouse, and Old Surry was sure that this was the case; and it was also said that Blingo, the blacksmith, attended these dark meetings.

There met two remarkable characters in the garden on this eventful night. Their faces were black as ebony, and each was a genius in her way. One of these was " Old Surry," the slave woman who had been given to Mrs.

Adams in 1765, and who refused her freedom when it
was offered to her later, and whose characteristics we
have already mentioned. The other was Phillis Wheatley,
who had achieved much local fame as a poet.   Phillis
came with Mrs. Wheatley, her mistress, whom she everywhere attended.

Old Surry, Mrs. Adams's maid, opened her eyes wide
and raised her black hands when she saw Phillis coming.
She seemed to wish to display the fact that she had advantages as well as the poor slave girl, whose poems had
become the wonder of the town.

" Sho', Phillis, am dat yo' ? "

" Yes, Sister Surry.   These are the times that make the
earth tremble.   I feel as though I must write another
poem now, like that which I sent to the king "

" Wot yo' sent to de king!   Don't yo' be proud of
no doin's like dat.   Yo' listen to me now.   I can't write
any poetry like yo', Phillis, but I can serb de greatest man
in all dese parts, and I would rather serb him dan weabe
a lot of ringlin', jinglin' rhymes for de greatest king on
earth.   I don't mean yo' no harm, Phillis.   Dat poetry
of yourn was real pretty, now, considerin' whar yo' come
from !   Phillis, how do yo' suppose yo' looked when I first
sot eyes on yo' ?   Why, yo' had nothin' but a coffee-bag
on yo' whole body, and yo' was bein' marched along wid
a parcel of Guinea slaves to be sold from de auction-block

jest like a cow. Whar would yo' ha' been if Mrs. Wheatley had not bought yo', and eddicated yo'? It is my duty to say dese things to keep yo' humble, Phillis."

The words of Old Surry were true. It was just in the manner described that Phillis Wheatley, whose early home had been in some unknown African wild, had entered Boston. She had been purchased by Mrs. Wheatley, who had already several slaves, but who wished to own a young negro girl, and to educate her that she might be a companion for her old age.

While Mrs. Wheatley was training this wild African girl, who could remember nothing of her parents except that she had seen her mother making offerings to the rising sun, a remarkable event had occurred in Boston. The Stamp Act, by which a duty had been imposed upon certain goods shipped to the colonies, and which was a heavy tax upon the colonies for the support of the crown, had been repealed. The colonies had suffered so much from the injustice of these stamp duties, and so resented the principle that the colonies might be taxed at the will of the crown without their consent and against their protest, without any representation in the government, that the news of the repeal of the Stamp Act was received in Boston town with the greatest joy; and the poor negro girl had caught the enthusiasm, and felt a thrill of gratitude toward the king, who, to her, represented marvellous kind-

4

ness, beneficence, and greatness of mind and soul.   It was
something wonderful to her to hear the cannon boom and
all the bells of Boston ringing.

The event which so excited her poetic fancy took place
on May 16 to May 19, 1766—three days that were like
one day in Boston town.   On May 16th a brigantine
named "The Harrison," six weeks from London, hove
into Boston Harbor, and bore the news that the Stamp
Act was repealed.   The bells of the city began to ring;
the shipping in the harbor was decked with colors; wood
was gathered for bonfires to be kindled on the hills; and
the people thronged the streets on that lovely May night,
and made merry under the Liberty Tree, under the old elm
on the Common, now gone, and under the Paddock Elms,
that stood near where Park Street Church now uplifts its
tall spire.   It was Saturday night.   The selectmen met
at Faneuil Hall as soon as the news came, and voted
that Monday should be a holiday and a time of general
rejoicing.

The Sabbath was a joyous thanksgiving.   The orchards
were in bloom; the great trees on the Common were
putting forth their leaves; the gardens were filled with
flowers.

The people were astir shortly after midnight on Monday
morning.   At one o'clock the bell of Dr. Byles's church
began to ring, close by the Liberty Tree.   It was answered
by the chimes of Christ Church on the hill, and then by

all the bells of the town. When the morning began to
dawn, the Hollis Street Church steeple appeared fluttering
with banners; the houses were gay with colors; drums
beat, and the cannon boomed. The Sons of Liberty resolved to set even the prisoners free, that they might share
in the joy; and they were able to do this through their
influence in the vice-regal councils.

At noon the Castle thundered; the guns were answered
by the battery of the town and that of Charlestown, by
the artillery, and by the guns on the ships in the harbor.

At night all the windows burst into flames, and fireworks filled the air. A pyramid had been erected on the
Common to contain two hundred and eighty lamps. The
elegant mansion of John Hancock, the richest man in the
town, was like a house of fire. He had spread a banquet
for the principal men of the town, and fireworks of extraordinary splendor filled the sky from the Hancock grounds
while the happy patriots dined. Until midnight the sky
upon the Common was red with rockets and wheels of fire.
Fifty-five lanterns illumined the Liberty Tree, and on the
following night one hundred and eight lamps were set like
fruit amid its branches.

The poor slave girl heard and saw all these scenes with
wonder; and to her the English king, in whose name all
this glory of parade and fire was made, seemed more like
a god than a man. Her excited imagination found relief
in poetry, of which the following lines are still preserved:

"Your subjects hope, dread sire, the crown,
Upon your brows may flourish long,
And that your arm may in your God be strong.
Oh! may your sceptre numerous nations sway,
And all with love and readiness obey.

"But how shall we the British king reward?
Rule thou in peace, our father and our lord!
'Midst the remembrance of thy favors past,
The meanest peasants most admire *the last*.
May George, beloved by all the nations round,
Live with heaven's choicest, constant blessings crowned.
Great God, direct and guard him from on high,
And from his head let every evil fly;
And may each clime with equal gladness see
A monarch's smile can set his subjects free."

The poem was greatly admired by the Boston friends of the Wheatleys, and was sent to the king.

The attention of the people in the garden on this night was suddenly called to a woman who came hurrying through the yard.

"De wife of one of dose Britishers," said Old Surry; "and what does she want of Massa Adams, for sho'?"

There had been some terrible whippings of the British soldiers on the Common. The punishments had been public, and two negroes of great strength had been selected to lay on the lashes. The agony of the victims had been extreme.

A large number of British soldiers had deserted, and

this caused the discipline in the two regiments to be made very severe.

The woman approached Mr. Adams.

" I am the wife of one of the soldiers," said she. " My husband is suspected of dissatisfaction. He is to be whipped by the negroes on the Common to-morrow morning— stripped and whipped before the regiment and crowd! Oh, Mr. Adams, I cannot endure it! You can save him!"

" I, madam?"

" Yes, you. Your words have power."

" In all the town of Boston there is no one who would have so little influence with the authorities in such a case as I. Madam, I pity you, but you have come to the wrong person."

" No, Mr. Adams, I have come to the right person. They respect you, they fear you, they know your influence. If you say that my husband shall not be whipped, he will not be whipped. The officers will go to the magistrates, and they will decide that they cannot afford to do such an act against the judgment and heart of Sam Adams. Mr. Adams, you are the town, you are the people, and these are serious times!"

Mr. Adams loved children, and pitied women in trouble. The " last of the Puritans," as he has been called, had a great heart.

He paced to and fro. 'He looked into the pleading face of the woman.

" Madam," he said, " I will see what I can do."

The next morning Mr. Adams rose early, and went to the officers' quarters. The woman was right: the council decided that it would not be wise to make an open enemy of Sam Adams. The two negroes stood ready at the appointed hour to inflict the punishment, but that soldier was never whipped.

This was the beginning of a series of events in which Mr. Adams's opinions and wishes had so much influence in the British military affairs that the soldiers sent for coercion came at last to be called not the army of the British crown, or governor, but " The Sam Adams Regiments." You shall be told how Sam Adams in bold, grand words caused them to be removed from Boston.

CHAPTER V.

THE DRUMMER-BOY.

ELL, my little drummer-boy, whom do you drum for?"

"Sam Adams, sir."

"Sam Adams? Who is this Sam Adams?"

"He's the moderator, sir."

"The moderator? What may that be?"

"Moderator of the folkmote, sir."

"And now have you come to drum for us?"

"No, sir, but I came to learn how to play that lively tune as you play it. I can play it now."

"Can you? Let me hear you."

The scene was the Town House, now the Old State House. The two persons who had thus become interested in each other were a British drummer and Allie.

Allie rattled away at the popular air.

The British drummer puffed out his cheeks, and said:

"Do I hear my ears? That is fine! You should drum for the king, my boy. You were born for it."

"I drum for Sam Adams, sir. I would like for you to drum the same tune."

"Give you a lesson? Then you will drum for the king?"

"No; I shall always drum for the cause, sir."

"For what cause, my boy?"

"For the American cause."

"For the Sons of Liberty?"

"Yes, sir."

"We intend, my boy, that the Sons of Liberty shall one day follow our drums, or else we shall drum them out of the town of Boston. Is this same Sam Adams one of the Sons of Liberty?"

"He is, sir."

"And you drum for him?"

"Yes, sir."

"Then we may have to drum him, and perhaps you, my boy, out of town. I would dislike to see you go— you are a likely boy, with spirit."

"It might be the other way, sir."

"How?"

"It might be I who should drum you, sir. Mr. Adams says that the place of the troops is at the Castle. He said in town-meeting that you have no right here in the Town House, and the governor must order the British regiments to leave the town."

"A very bold man is this same Sam Adams. And you

drum for him, and think that you may live to drum us out of town! And you have come to ask me to give you a lesson! Is this the way that you would like to play when you see us going?"

The Britisher played " Nancy Dawson " with great vigor. Allie mastered the future " Yankee Doodle," and repeated it after him.

"You have learned *your* lesson well, my boy. Now which in the end will drum the other out of town?"

" I'm obliged to you for the lesson," said Allie.

" You are a little rebel," laughed the British drummer.

" Yes, sir, but I can drum."

The two sat at the front door of the Town House, under the arms of England, which may still be seen there. In the halls above the British soldiers were sleeping, reading, or playing games. The British flag floated over the house, and before the door stood two cannon pointed toward the building.

The old State House, then the Town House, is a museum now. It is opened each day to the public, free, and my reader only needs to visit it to live for two generations in a single day. I love to sit down in the old council-chamber, or in the Hancock room, and think. At one end of the building is a great window and small balcony, from which the Georges were proclaimed kings, and the royal governors first faced their new subjects amid salvos of artillery. Under that window the first blood of the

Revolution was shed in the so-called Boston massacre.
There Crispus Attucks, whose monument can be seen on
the Common, fell.

In the Hall of Representatives here Sam Adams first
recommended that the American colonies unite a common
cause for liberty.   Here he proclaimed the principle that
taxation without representation was injustice, and that the
colony should not allow itself to be taxed without the
consent of the assembly.   Here he asserted the first principles of the Declaration of Independence.

The old State House is a congress of original portraits,
and there pictures of nearly all the ancient houses of Boston may be seen.   The thrilling portrait of Sam Adams
by Copley is in the Art Museum, but the grand patriot
haunted the Town House for nearly fifty years, and his
spirit seems to linger there.   In these hallowed rooms
may be seen the old clock of Mather Byles; a snare-drum
beaten at Bunker Hill; the Hancock Bible and prayer-
book, and the knocker on John Hancock's door; his canes,
slippers, pew-books, pocketbooks, and even his pepper-
box; the fan of romantic Agnes Surriage (Lady Frank-
land); the once famous crewel embroidery of the Hancock
house, with Governor Hancock on horseback, proudly riding before it, and Dorothy, his wife, looking over the wall
toward the Charles River; a picture of General Gage and
the Boston boys; and more than a thousand curiosities
associated for the most part with heroic colonial times.

The fireplace remains as in former times, and the lion and the unicorn still seem about to spring from the outside roof.

As Allie stood in the council-chamber, where a little later Sam Adams was to shake the empire, the British drummer said to an officer:

"See, here is a boy who drums for Sam Adams."

"Well, my boy, you will not have to drum long. That man has nearly gotten through with his head; the king will have need of it soon."

He lifted his hand as though about to sever his head, as a sign of what would befall Sam Adams. Allie gazed at him for a moment in horror, and then fled down the stairs into the street.

As he came home he saw that a crowd had gathered on the Purchase Street side of Mr. Adams's garden. With them was the patriot schoolmaster. Mr. Adams was walking to and fro, with his hands behind him. After what the officer had said, Allie looked up at the silent, absent-minded man in a kind of awe.

He gazed into the powerful face. His mind was filled with an anxious fear as he saw the patriot raise his hand and, turning to Master Holbrooke, say:

"I am all alone. *They* are thinking only of securing a redress of their grievances; *I* am not thinking of that. *They* are thinking of charter rights; Master Holbrooke, I am longing to see these colonies unite and become inde-

pendent and free. Independent, Master Holbrooke, independent! I would die to see them independent! "

The master held the same views. Sam Adams walked
to and fro again, his dog following at his heels.

Old Surry sat there gazing at him, with a look of wonder in her eyes.

" I alone of all the people dare to talk openly of independence," added the statesman.

" De Lord takes possession of dat man sometimes," said
Old Surry. " Allie, you beat out dat new tune on de
drum, and bring him down from de mount."

The little drum rolled through the garden, and Sam
Adams held out his hand toward the boy, and said:

" I love music and children, and—the cause. But my
cause is not like others. Independence—independence—
independence!"

He was in the prime of life—gray, but grand and full
of strength. James K. Hosmer, in his " Life of Samuel
Adams," presents a picture of his home at this time which
is very simple, sympathetic, and beautiful, and such as
might lead a poet or a writer of fiction to enlarge upon it.
It is as follows:

" He still occupied the house on Purchase Street. . . .
It was a sightly place, from which stretched seaward before the eye the island-studded harbor, with the many
ships; the bastions of the Castle, low lying to the right;
and landward, the town, rising fair upon the hills. Samuel

Adams, shortly before this time, had been able, probably with the help of friends, to put his home in good order, and managed to be hospitable. For apparently life went forward in his home, if frugally, not parsimoniously, his admirable wife making it possible for him, from his small income as clerk of the House, to maintain a decent house-keeping. His son, now twenty-two years old, was studying medicine with Dr. Warren, after a course at Harvard, a young man for whom much could be hoped. His daughter was a promising girl of seventeen. With the young people and their intimates the father was cordial and genial. He had an ear for music and a pleasant voice in singing, a recreation which he much enjoyed. The house was strictly religious; grace was said at each meal, and the Bible is still preserved from which some member of the household read aloud each night. Old Surry, a slave woman given to Mrs. Adams in 1765, and who was freed upon coming into her possession, lived in the family nearly fifty years, showing devoted attachment. When slavery was abolished in Massachusetts, papers of manumission were made out for her in due form; but these she threw into the fire in anger, saying she had lived too long to be trifled with. The servant-boy whom Samuel Adams carefully and kindly reared became afterward a mechanic of character, and worked efficiently in his former master's behalf when at length in old age Adams was proposed for governor. Nor must Queue be forgotten, the big, intelligent Newfoundland dog, who appreciated perfectly what was due to his position as the dog of Sam Adams. He had a great antipathy to the British uniform. He was cut and shot in several places by soldiers, in retaliation for his own sharp attacks; for the patriotic Queue anticipated even the 'embattled farmers' of Concord Bridge in inaugurating hostilities, and bore to his grave honorable scars from his fierce encounters."

This man, of all the leaders of the colonies, stood at this time almost alone in his one dream of American independence. The other statesmen only sought to obtain the rights of the people under the crown.

Was there ever in America a figure more grand than this man in his loneliness, dreaming dreams which were to become maps of all the future? We love to think of him in these lonely days.

CHAPTER VI.

HE two British regiments in Boston became
known in history as "The Sam Adams Regiments," because Sam Adams at last made them
subject to his own orders. It is a curious story and a
noble one, and we must follow it here through a series of
thrilling and wonderful events.

The boys of the West School all liked to follow the new
tune of Allie Fayreweather's drum. War was in the air,
and they spent their pastimes in building snow-forts, and
fighting snow-ball battles on the Common. The boys of
the West School were led by Allie Fayreweather's drum
in their assaults on the snow-forts of their companions in
other schools, on School Street and elsewhere. The roll
of this drum was usually a call to victory.

So the mimic war went on around the Frog Pond,
under the bare old elm and the great elms on the Park
Street Mall. The forts of the schools grew in strength
and space, and at last attracted the attention of the British

49

troops. The British officers seemed to read treason in their battles of the snow-balls.

Above the Frog Pond is slanting ground, and here the boys raised hills of snow to carry their sleds with greater momentum across the ice of the pond. The British soldiers felt that these boys were their enemies, and they in a certain sense began the war of the Revolution by making covert and cowardly attacks on these same hills. The boys would erect their snow planes on one day to find that they had been destroyed on the next day; beaten down at night or in school hours by the muskets of soldiers belonging to the two British regiments.

The boys of the West School and other schools held a council. What ought they to do? Should they go to Sam Adams, who governed the town in spite of all British authority, and who was a friend of boys?

" Go to General Gage himself and demand justice and satisfaction," said Philip Fayreweather.

"And I will beat the drum," said Allie.

To follow the old legend, which has found representation in art (see print of " General Gage and the Boston Boys," Old State House), the boys went to the Province House, which stood nearly opposite the Old South Church, and a small part of whose wall, built into another building, is still sometimes chipped by relic-hunters. It was a grand house in its day, and had once belonged to Lady Phips, whose husband, Sir William, had been enriched and

knighted by finding a Spanish ship of gold sunken off
the Bahama Islands. Hawthorne, in his "Legends of the
Province House," has told the stories and legends of this
seat of the administration of most of the ten royal governors. No New England stories are as strange and pic-
turesque as those. They are haunting, especially "Old
Hester Dudley" and "Lady Eleanor's Mantle"—tales fit
for Hallowe'en.

General Gage, if we may follow the pictures, stood in
the door of the mansion, and was greatly surprised to see
a company of boys approaching him, followed by nearly
all the children of the town.

"What brings you here?" he asked of the leader, who
stopped before the steps under the royal arms.

"We have come, sir,"—to use the language of the
original legend—"we have come, sir, to demand satisfaction."

"Demand satisfaction!" Those were strong, Sam-
Adams-like words, and if they were indeed used, the
haughty general must have felt their force even though
he met them in a derisive way.

"What!" said General Gage. "Have your fathers
been teaching you rebellion, and sent you to exhibit it
here?"

"No one sent us, sir. We have come of our own will.
We have never done injury to your troops, but they break
down our snow-hills and destroy our skating-grounds.

5

We complained, and what did they call us? Young rebels, and laughed at our rights. We went to the captain. He, too, laughed at us, and now we have come to appeal to you for protection and justice."

The general was touched by the manliness of the appeal. He is said to have uttered the fine sentiment to one of his officers—" The very children draw in the love of liberty in the air they breathe."

" I will see that your playground is protected," said he.

Allie hurried back to the schoolhouse, his little drum beating more lively than ever before. The German boy, Snyder, was with him, and they were met at the door by the patriot schoolmaster.

" Victory !" shouted the little drummer-boy, and he told the tale of the conference in the Province House yard. " The boys have won the victory," he said at the end; and then rattled away at the new tune, while the other boys came back in high spirits.

An awful event followed. The first person to fall in the War of the Revolution was not Crispus Attucks, but a boy. If Attucks, who fell by an accidental encounter, merits a monument as the first who fell for liberty, so does this boy.

There were a few merchants in Boston who continued to sell taxed articles. They came to be despised and hated. Among these was one Theophilus Lillie. The boys in their hasty patriotism made on a placard a list of the names of those who imported and sold proscribed articles, and put it upon a pole that bore a wooden head and hand.

It was a queer-looking object. The boys bore it aloft in the air, and carried it through the town. Allie followed them with his drum, accompanied by Snyder, the patriotic German boy. When the crowd of boys reached the business establishment of Lillie, they set the queer image up before the importer's door, with the wooden hand pointing toward it, at the same time laughing and jeering and making merry.

Lillie came to the door, saw the image, and became very angry.

The boys remained in the street, before Lillie's door. The jeers became changed into hard language.

A countryman came along the street on a great cart, and a man by the name of Richardson, a friend of the importer, tried to get him to drive against the image and break it down.

" Never!" said the countryman. " I am for the people."

Richardson was a Tory, and began to try to break down the grotesque image. The boys had lost their good sense, and pelted him with snow, mud, and stones.

Richardson was very angry. He rushed into a house, and brought out a musket. He aimed it at the boys, and fired.

A boy named Christopher Gore, afterward Governor of

Massachusetts, was slightly wounded. Presently there
was a hush. Little Christopher Snyder, Allie's friend, a
boy whose mother was a widow, and who had followed
the spirit of the times, fell, mortally wounded. They took
up his form and bore it away, and the whole city wept.

Never in America was there a boy's funeral like his.
They made for him a patriot's coffin, and bore his form to
the Liberty Tree, which stood near the present corner of
Washington and Essex Streets. On the coffin was this
motto: " Innocence itself is not safe."

The tree was near the West Schoolhouse. Four of the
boy's companions, among them Allie, were selected to be
his bearers. The boys of nearly all the schools, some six
hundred in number, gathered around the body as an
escort. The bells tolled; business was closed, and some
fifteen hundred people followed the first martyr to the
grave.

As the procession marched, not only the bells of Boston but those of the neighboring towns were heard tolling. It was almost spring, and there was a mellowness in
the air. That procession was a prophecy of events to come,
a protest against the injustice of the royal power. The
Sons of Liberty should remember little Snyder's grave.

The wheels of destiny were moving fast now. Darker
tragedies were at hand. The citizens became so hostile
to the British soldiers that many of them expressed their
contempt for them as they passed them in the street.

On the first Friday in March a British soldier had a quarrel with some rope-makers. He was beaten, but returned to the barracks, secured the help of his comrades, and beat. the rope-makers. The affair filled the town with excitement, and the rope-makers resolved after the Sabbath to have their revenge.

It was Monday evening, March 5, 1770. The toils of the day were over, and excited people everywhere filled the streets.

About seven o'clock in the evening a crowd of some seven hundred men assembled in King's Street, now State Street, around the Town House, now the old State House. They began shouting:

"Drive out the rascals! They have no right here; drive them out! "

The body of men grew. By nine o'clock it numbered a large part of the men of the town.

They gathered around the British soldiers in Dock Square, shouting:

"Turn them out, turn them out!" "Down with the bloody soldiers!" "Drive them out!"

A cry of fire in the streets set the bells of the town to ringing. The whole population was awake, and the hours of the March night wore on, each one bringing new excitements.

In Dock Square there occurred a very extraordinary thing, ghost-like and strange, which no one has ever explained. A mysterious stranger made his way through the crowd. He was very tall; he was dressed in scarlet, and he wore a white wig. He seemed on this March night like a prophet, like a new Castor and Pollux, or the ghost of Hadley—some one sent out of the regions unknown. All eyes were bent on his white head and tall form.

He began to speak. His words were like swords of fire. Suddenly, as the crowd in the shadows stood in awe, he shouted:

" To the main guard!   To the main guard!"

" To the main guard!   To the main guard!" echoed the people. The crowd began to surge and move, and the mysterious stranger disappeared. Can any boy in the Boston schools tell us who this man was? It was his order that in fact began the Revolution.

The crowd moved on the main guard, pressing upon the soldiers, denouncing and threatening them.

Among them was Crispus Attucks, at the head of a party of sailors. He was a colored man. He took up the cry of the multitude and shouted: " To the main guard! To the main guard!"

The soldiers loaded their guns.

" You dare not fire!" cried Attucks.

The crowd pressed to the very points of the bayonets.

" Come on!" shouted Attucks. " Come on! They dare not fire!"

Captain Pearson came up and endeavored to appease

the multitude.   Attucks aimed a blow at his head, but instead of felling the officer, he struck the musket of one of the soldiers to the ground.   He attempted to seize the musket.   A struggle with the owner ensued.

"Fire!" shouted voices from some unknown quarter.

The soldier who was·struggling with Attucks was named Montgomery.   He heard the word "Fire!" and wrenched his musket from the mulatto.

Flash!

Attucks fell dead.   He was, after Snyder, the second patriot to fall.   They buried him, and his grave used to be seen where once stood the larch-tree in the Granary Burying-ground, near the present Tremont House.

What a night was there beneath the moon and stars! Other shots were fired, and three of the populace were killed and five were wounded.

"Turn out with your arms!" shouted the people. "Let the alarm drums beat!"   "To arms! to arms!"

The moon was in her first quarter, and shone faintly over the bloody snow under the balcony of the Town House, and over the dark forms hurrying everywhere through the streets.

The boys who had sworn to protect the guns in the gun-house hurried thither.   But there was no need of a guard.   The small hours of the night passed, and a meeting of the Sons of Liberty in Faneuil Hall had been summoned for the morning.

And where were Sam Adams and little Allie during these exciting scenes? The man of the town-meeting, who would make a republic out of the town-meeting, was hastening to and fro, and saying, "The regiments must go." And to that decision responded the drum of his little companion—"Rub-a-dub-dub, rub-dub-dub!"

The next day the people met in various assemblies. The country folks came pouring into the city. There was a great meeting in Faneuil Hall in the morning, and Samuel Adams was appointed one of a committee of fifteen to go to the royal governor and demand the removal of the troops from the town. Whom were the two regiments now to obey, the governor, or Sam Adams, the commoner?

The committee met Governor Hutchinson and the commanding officer, General Dalrymple, and made their demand.

"I have no authority in the matter," said the governor. "The troops are subject to the orders of General Gage."

An appeal was made to General Dalrymple.

"I have only the authority to remove one regiment," he replied. "According to General Gage's order the Twenty-ninth Regiment was to be placed at the Castle. That regiment may go to the Castle. For the other regiment I can only await the orders of General Gage."

The committee issued out of the doors of the Town

House to make their report at the meeting of the citizens in the Old South Church.

Sam Adams led the way. He was America, as it were, all alone.

As he marched along from the Town House to the Old South Church he seemed lost in thought. The people stared at him.

"Both regiments or none; both regiments or none!" he kept saying, as though there were no one near to hear. "Both regiments or none; both regiments or none!"

The Old South Church was thronged with excited people: the aisles, stairs, and entrances.

The reply of the governor was made to the people— that one regiment might be removed.

Suddenly the crowd broke forth in a tumultuous voice. What was it? It was the sentence of Sam Adams as he talked to himself on the street:

"Both regiments or none!"

The house shook. "Both regiments or none!"

A committee of seven were appointed to go back to the governor and repeat the demand that both regiments be removed. The first name on this committee was John Hancock, the second was Sam Adams.

The day was waning as the committee of seven went to the council-chamber in the Town House. Sam Adams was the spokesman, and he uttered words that will never die. Copley's portrait in the Art Museum, Boston, rep-

resents Sam Adams in this thrilling scene. Picture the
council-chamber, its March fire and dim lights. Before
the table, surrounded by royal portraits, sat the governor
and his officers. Scarlet and gold lace and official dignity were there.

Grandly, in simple garb, Sam Adams confronted the
vice-royal array. His words were like the sweep of the
hurricane, thrilling and unanswerable. He said:

"It is well known that, acting as governor of the province, you are by its charter the commander-in-chief of the
military forces within it; and as such, the troops now in
the capital are subject to your orders. If you, or General
Dalrymple under you, have the *power to remove one regiment, you have the power to remove both;* and nothing
short of their total removal will satisfy the people, or pre-
serve the peace of the province. A multitude highly in-
censed now wait the result of this application. The voice
of ten thousand freemen demands that both regiments be
forthwith removed. Their voice must be respected, their
demand obeyed. Fail not then, at your peril, to comply
with this requisition! On you alone rests the responsi-
bility of this decision; and if the just expectations of the
people are disappointed, you must be answerable to God
and your country for the fatal consequences that must
ensue. The committee have discharged their duty, and
it is for you to discharge yours. They wait your final
determination!"

If you have power to remove one to insert, you have power to ...

He trembled as he spoke. The governor himself was seen to tremble. A conference between the governor and General Dalrymple followed. The governor yielded. The regiments should go.

They were "Sam Adams's regiments," said an English lord in derision, and so they came to be called. Sam Adams, as it were, had won the cause of liberty for all America and all lands. We love the council-chamber of the old State House, and the curious pictures of Sam Adams there.

The guns in the gun-house were safe now, and would be likely to remain so for a long time to come. But they only waited a thrilling history.

As Sam Adams came home after that most eventful day of his life, he was met by little Allie and "good Old Surry," as he was accustomed to call the colored woman.

"Are dey gwine?" said the latter.

"Yes, Surry, they are going."

"You sent them away?"

"They are going."

"Bress all de hebbens! You Allie, you, play dat dar new tune."

If my reader lives in Boston, let him go to the Art Museum to look at the portrait of Sam Adams, one of the noblest representations of an animated, heroic face in all America. It hangs near to Stuart's Washington. It has a beautiful history. Adams and Hancock at one time

became estranged, and Hancock had this grand portrait of
Adams and another of himself painted, which now hangs
beside it, to commemorate their reconciliation. After
Stuart's Washington, there is no portrait in America that
I so much like to see. One may almost hear it speaking
the words quoted in this chapter. It is the portrait of an
event and a soul. Every boy or girl who visits Boston
should go to see it. It stands for the pivotal point of
human liberty.

CHAPTER VII.

THE town-meetings were the great events of the colony now. As the people were allowed to debate every question, they were not only generally instructive, but were often amusing. Old Boston used to be full of anecdotes of the town-meetings.

The most thrilling of all town-meetings is that which we are about to picture. But before we give an account of this in narrative form, let us glance at one of lighter features. Almost every town-meeting had its character, a man of peculiar traits, who delighted to be heard and felt. We will attempt to picture one of these.

The town-meeting day came. The meeting was to be held in Faneuil Hall. The same hall is now opened daily to the public, over the market that fronts the square in which stands the long Quincy Market building. It is only a little way from the old State House and the Old South Church, both of which are also opened to the public daily as historic museums. So much of this story is historically true that I will be pleased if my reader on visiting Boston

will go to see the Old South Church of Warren, the old
State House of Sam Adams, and Faneuil Hall, in whose
folkmoot the free government of America was born, or, if
it were born rather in the compact of the "Mayflower,"
received its primitive education.

The bells of the churches rang to remind the townspeople of their duties.   As the principal topic to be dis-
cussed· was higher education, or classical education, the
boys as well as the freeholders were interested in this
special meeting.   It was known that Dr. Oliver was to
oppose classical education in the public schools, and the
doctor could not bear boys, and he was as unpopular
among the schools as Sam Adams was loved and admired.

The meeting assembled at ten o'clock in the morning.
The townsmen began to gather early, and with them most
of the boys of the schools.   Sam Adams, brusque and
portly, entered the hall and took his seat near the place
where the great picture of "Webster's Reply to Hayne"
now hangs.   The reader may find most of the portraits
of the leaders of the Old Boston town-meeting in colonial
days hanging about different parts of the hall.

The venerable clerk, Mr. Cooper, who had kept the
town records for many years, sat at the moderator's desk,
with a number of great books before him.

" The first business of the meeting," said the clerk, rising with a grave air, "is to choose a moderator.   Whom
do you nominate?"

"Sam Adams," said many voices. There was a silence, amid which rose a piping voice.

"I don't." It was Dr. Oliver.

"Is the motion seconded?"

There was a murmur of "I second the motion" from all parts of the hall. The same piping voice rose again.

"I don't."

"The motion is made and seconded that Samuel Adams act as moderator of this meeting. If that be your pleasure say 'aye.'"

"I move that there be a ballot." It was Dr. Oliver.

"It is moved that there be a ballot. Is the motion seconded?"

There was a dead silence.

"Somebody second the motion," said Dr. Oliver. "Isn't there any *other* man here who has some common sense?"

But the motion failed, and Sam Adams was almost unanimously elected moderator. Dr. Oliver heard the clerk announce the result with a disgust that nearly turned his big wig. He sank down on his cane, saying:

"I expect nothing else but that I'll have to quit my country."

After some simple business had been transacted without opposition, Master Holbrooke introduced the following resolution:

"Be it resolved by the townsmen of Boston in town-

meeting assembled, that it is the sense of this assembly of
freeholders that a course of classical studies, which shall
offer our sons and daughters a clear knowledge of Latin
and Greek, is a necessary part of our system of free education." The motion was seconded by many voices.

Dr. Oliver rose on his cane. His form was tall, but
bent.

"Mr. Moderator," he exclaimed, "a few people have
had their way in this town long enough, and now it is
time that *I* had my say. I am not to be deterred any
longer. My position on education is this: let a select few
be thoroughly educated, and let them be education for
all. That is the way learning flourished in the middle
ages, in the days of Alfred the Great and of Charlemagne.
That is common sense. Now you have had your own
wills, and I will have my own will—it is my right, and I
will."

"You shall," said a number of voices. "We'll make
you!"

"Sirs, this is an outrage. I was about to say that if all
the sons of the rabble are to be taught Latin and Greek,
the time has come for me to quit my country. Let those
be educated who have the greatest capacity and leisure,
for the sake of the whole people. That is sense. Educate
everybody—that is mob rule. Class education means
thrift; universal education, idleness. Sam Adams, you
love boys and girls of all classes. I don't. The best

should lead—that is common sense—you can see it is! Sam Adams, Sam Adams, where are we tending?"

"May it please your honor," we may suppose Sam Adams to have said, for such were his views, "we are tending to become a free nation, whose very foundation must be public education. When time shall have made the whole nation one grand town-meeting, we shall have only the virtue of the people to sustain our government; and the foundation of public enlightenment is education, and knowledge should be free as the water and the air."

"Then I will quit my country. Who would live with an impudent educated rabble? I would rather quit my country. I will, and I will do as I have a mind to."

"You shall!" shouted the people and the boys.

"I will!" thundered Dr. Oliver, majestically swinging his cane.

"We'll make you!" said a dozen men.

"No, you shall not! Make me have my own will! I'd like to see the men who can make me do it!"

"Call a vote on the question," cried a voice.

The doctor swung his cane high in the air, and sat down with red face, in a high state of nervous excitement, remarking to his friends that Sam Adams was a "rebel," and would lose his head some day. Odd episodes similar to this were very common in the free old town-meeting days.

It was the town-meeting that was called to prevent the

6

landing of the taxed tea, a part of which had come over on the ship "Dartmouth," that was the power that shook the British empire in the West.

Lonely old Sam Adams watched its approach. The people everywhere were talking of a "redress of their wrongs" and the "maintainment of their rights and privileges under the crown." These words were to him as children's tales. He looked beyond such views. He saw events were tending to a greater conception of the rights and privileges of the colonies. He was dreaming always of a free nation as the outcome of the agitations around him. And so he walked the streets of Boston, dreaming, dreaming, forgetful of his business, forgetful of his home, lonely, lonely, mysterious, living in the future. So all the Heaven-inspired leaders of men have walked their lonely ways.

The great town-meeting day of all! How shall we describe it? Let us tell the story as Allie related it to excited Old Surry that day.

"Mis' Fayreweather, come here! De lan'! de lan'!" So cried Old Surry to her neighbor on the afternoon of the great town-meeting.

"What is it?" asked Mrs. Fayreweather.

"Come here! Come here! De lan'! de lan'!"

Old Surry's eyes had never seemed so large and white before. They rolled hither and thither. Mrs. Fayreweather crossed the street nervously.

"What is it, Surry?"

"Wot you seen? Injuns? Have you seen Injuns? I has. Where's yo' boys?"

"Where did you see Indians, Surry?"

"Mis' Fayreweather, fo' de law, I see an Injun come out yo' own door—Heaben clap me into nothin'—like a chicken-hawk a peepin' chicken when he swoop down, a shadow, and woe be to de chicken!—if I tell any lie! His face was black—black as Phillis's; and he had on a red blanket, and he carried a hatchet in his hand, and didn't walk, but glided along like de ghost of one of de dead pirates when de Ebil One am arter him. O Mis' Fayreweather, that ain't all! Phillis, she's been ober here, and she's seen Injuns! An' what kind o' doin's hab dey been habin' in de Ole South Church? De lan'! de lan'! well may I ask yo' dat! Dere comes yo' drummer-boy now. He's been dar. Here, yo' Sam Adams's boy, yo' come here. What yo' seen? What yo' hear?"

The day was cold, still, and clear; a fireless day of December, chill, but not severe. The excitement in the town was such that few regarded the weather, and the two women and the boy stood there in the evening air thinking only of the events of the day.

It was December 16th, the crisis day of liberty. Thousands of people crowded the Old South Church; it is said that two thousand came in from the country towns. The bells rang for that meeting as for an assembly of fate.

Samuel Phillips Savage, of Weston, was chairman. The resolution of this great meeting was that the ships with the taxed tea should be sent back to England.

There had been a conference between the committee of the town and Mr. Francis Rotch, the owner of the " Dartmouth," the principal tea ship, concerning the sending back of the tea. The committee went with Mr. Rotch to the collector, and the collector promised to return an answer on this day, the 16th of December.

The answer came, early in the meeting. It thrilled the assembly.

" I have received my orders from the collector," said Mr. Rotch. " He will not grant a clearance to my ship."

That meant that the taxed tea should be landed when an opportunity favored, or announced to the people the principle that the crown asserted the right to land the taxed tea.

The answer of the town-meeting to the importer was terrible—in substance this:

" Go get your ship ready for sea this day, utter your protest against the custom-house, and proceed directly to the governor [then at Milton] and demand a pass for your ship to go under the guns of the Castle."

Mr. Rotch hastened to obey. The town-meeting adjoined till three o'clock to await his report.

The meeting assembled in the Old South Church at three o'clock. Josiah Quincy was the orator, in those days of orators. An hour passed, and Mr. Rotch did not return. The oration was over, and the great assembly of patriots waited. The town knew that delay meant denial. Every moment seemed one of fate.

At a quarter before six o'clock Mr. Rotch returned. Men hardly dared to breathe. Was it the town-meeting or the crown? Which was the power that governed the colony? Whose was the town of Boston—George III.'s or Sam Adams's, the uncrowned king representing the people?

Mr. Rotch would answer for the royal governor.

"For the honor of the laws, and from my duty to the king, I cannot grant the permit for the ship to pass the Castle until she is cleared by the regular authorities."

"Mr. Rotch," demanded the committee, "would you land that tea if you were ordered to do so by any authority?"

"I would be obliged to do so if I were so ordered by the regular authorities," was the decisive answer.

It was about to be moved that the meeting adjourn, when a wild cry rent the air. It was a war-whoop. It came from outside the church. There was a thrill of excitement. Sam Adams rose to allay it. It was already dark. Was the war-whoop a call? There were "Indians" in the street, running hither and thither. The town-meeting adjourned. There were more "Indians" in the street;

mysterious forms were everywhere. Where were Adams and Hancock? Why did not husbands and sons return to their homes?

"Boy," said Old Surry to Allie, "yo' come right into de kitchen wid yo' mudder now. De lan'! de lan'! Wot times dese be! Injuns in de air, Injuns scootin', no one knows whar. Yo' follow me."

The three sat down before the fire.

"Now what did yo' see at de town-meetin', boy, in de Ole South Church? Is the ship gwine to sail?"

"No."

"Den dar'll be war shure's you'se bawn. Now tell us, wot did yo' hear?"

"The governor answered 'No,' and then somebody shouted somewhere, all in the dark as it were—'Boston Harbor will be a teapot to-night.'"

"It wasn't Mr. Adams dat shouted dat, was it?"

"No, it was mysterious—came out of the air, as it were. It was getting dark."

"It was de voice ob de Lawd. Dat's wot it was. It was de voice ob de Lawd."

"And, mother, the town is full of Indians—Mohawks."

"Dar, Mis' Fayreweather, wot dat I tell yo'? Wot are dose Injuns here fo'?"

"They are come to destroy the tea. They are town-meeting Indians."

"Town-meetin' Injuns! De town-meetin' don't make

Injuns, do it? Boy, whar' am Mr. Adams? Yo' had oughter know."

" He sent me home."

" He did? "

" Yes, he told me not to wait for him to-night; he said that he would not be at home to *tea*."

The Widow Fayreweather went home, across the way. Her two older boys were not there. Except to the evening-school and to Mr. Adams's, they seldom went abroad without telling her where they were going. She felt lonely on this exciting night, and she returned to Mr. Adams's. Phillis Wheatley was still there, greatly excited.

" I wish," said the widow, " that you would all come over to my house, and pass an hour or two with me until the boys come home. Mrs. Adams has company, but Allie and I will be all alone."

" Dat we will," said good Old Surry. " Phillis, yo' come. Dis is a night ob wonders."

Poor Phillis's eyes were full of silent excitement. Old Surry crossed the street after the widow and Allie, and Phillis followed them.

They sat down around a dying fire to tell stories, and to prophesy, for both Old Surry and Phillis were prophetic in their way. Old Surry began to utter wild and fearful words.

" When," said she, lifting her hands and swinging them in a circle around her white turban—" when I see Massa

Adams a-walkin' around *so* "—here she arose and put her
hands behind her, and lifted her face toward the ceiling—
"and sayin' nothin', only utterin' mysterious words, as
though he war talkin' with de spirit ob de departed, I tink
—shall I tell yo' wot I tink?   I tink dis now—yo' listen
—I tink his soul soar away "—here she swung up her
great arms—" I tink his soul soar away, an' go like Moses
up into the Mount ob Vision, and I tink dat he see things,
revealed to him, like.   I once heard him say something
about dat he must make all things like de ' pattern showed
to him in de mount.'   Massa Adams, he forget things.
I tink these be the last times, or that something dreadful
is goin' to happen.   How do yo' know them are live Injuns?   How yo' know but de dead Injuns are risin' already?   Wot if one ob dem Injuns were to appear wid
fedders on his head, wot——"

Just here, as Old Surry was walking about the room in
a state of imaginary terrors, the door slowly opened, and
she looked toward it, and threw up her arms as one transfixed.   Phillis glanced toward the door, and hid behind
Mrs. Fayreweather's chair, peeping at times with wild
eyes over the top.   Mrs. Fayreweather arose, and Allie
stood beside her, wondering.

The door opened more widely.   An Indian stood before them, tall, ochre-faced, with blanket and feathers.

" All de heabens sabe us now—de day ob reckoning

am come at last!" Old Surry here uttered a fearful shriek, which was echoed by Phillis.

"Sir," said Mrs. Fayreweather, "what does this mean?"

"It means, *mother*, that the tea on the 'Dartmouth' has all been thrown overboard, and is now floating in Boston Harbor. It was the *Mohawks* who did it, and I was one of the Mohawks."

"Philip Fayreweather, is this right?" said Mrs. Fayreweather.

"Am dat right?" fiercely demanded Old Surry. "Am dat right?"

Phillis now stood up behind the chair.

"I guess it is all right," said Philip.

"Where am Massa Adams?" demanded Old Surry.

"I think he was there," said Philip. "I know that John Hancock was, for I knew him by his ruffles."

Philip threw off his blanket. He then untied his shoes, and poured out a quantity of sweet-smelling tea.

"Let us have a cup of tea," said Allie.

"Never!" said Mrs. Fayreweather.

The widow took her broom, and swept the tea into the fire.

The door opened again, and another Indian appeared. It was Andrew. Allie seized his drum.

"Has Mr. Adams returned?" he asked.

"Yes," said Andrew; "he is just going into the yard."

Allie opened the door, and the lively new tune rolled through the air. Amid its music Old Surry and Phillis fled across the street, and entered the door with the "American Cromwell," who stopped for a moment to listen to little Allie:

"Rub-a-dub-dub, rub-a-dub."

CHAPTER VIII.

HERE were two rumors in the air: one was that General Gage had tried to reconcile Sam Adams to the crown, and had failed, and was about to arrest him and send him to England to be tried for treason; another was that he was about to seize all the arms belonging to the Sons of Liberty.

The last rumor caused a meeting of the young committee of seven. They consulted with the Sons of Liberty. It was resolved to set a night-watch over the guns in the gun-house. Who should it be? It was decided to try little Allie with his drum.

It was examination-day at the writing-school.

Dr. Oliver stood before the West Schoolhouse, in cocked hat, gold-laced vest, and velvet coat, his bosom and wrists white with ruffles. He was a plump, prosperous, elderly man, who was opposed to progress, and who believed that the world was created for the privileged classes. He was bitterly opposed to the views of Sam Adams. He had been chosen with Mr. Adams to exer-

cise supervision over the West School, and it was in virtue
of this office that he was now here.

Samuel Adams was seen approaching the place. Plainly
dressed, he came slowly up to the common schoolhouse,
his dog following him. Behind was Allie with his drum.
Dr. Oliver had conceived a special dislike to Allie, whom
he was accustomed to call " Sam Adams's boy."

Master Holbrooke appeared at the door of the schoolhouse. It was a melting April day. The blue sky seemed
to prophesy the mild season of balm and bloom ; the blue-
birds were filling the budding leafy boughs of the trees
with cheerful notes.

Elegant Dr. Oliver and plain Sam Adams met at the
door of the schoolhouse. Dr. Oliver greeted the latter
coolly, and said :

" Mr. Adams, you have had an interview with General
Gage, I hear."

" Yes, sir, he sent for me."

" He did you great honor, and I hear that he asked you
to make peace with the king."

" He did so, my friend."

" That was very gracious. And what did you say ? "

" I told him that I had made my peace with the King
of kings."

" And he offered to treat you generously, did he not ? "

" He did."

" And did you not accept his proffer of favors ? "

" No; I told him plainly that no personal consideration should ever induce me to abandon the righteous cause of my country."

" Sam Adams, let me tell you plainly, your life has always been a failure, and so it will ever be."

" I have failed in the things to which I never was called."

" You tried to keep a tavern, and failed."

" I never was called to keep a tavern."

" You tried to be a tax-collector, and failed."

" Out of sympathy for the people."

" You had to follow your father's business, and failed."

" My heart was set on more useful things."

" Will you tell me what you can do, and not fail? "

" Right."

" He can conduct a town-meeting," said little Allie, almost crying for pity, with a rub-a-dub-dub on his drum.

Dr. Oliver turned toward the boy and glared at him.

" You little sass-box, you are a product of the times! No one has said anything to you, and the first lesson that you should learn is silence in the presence of your superiors. Master Holbrooke, there is a fine illustration of the new education."

" I beg your pardon, sir," said Allie.

" Silence!" thundered the doctor. " A man who cannot run a tavern never was called to run a town, much less a nation."

Sam Adams did not resent these hard words. He had heard such before. He only said:

"Covet earnestly the best gifts. The future tells the truth about all things."

The people were gathering around the schoolhouse, waiting for the bell to ring.

Suddenly Dr. Oliver turned toward Allie, and said:

"Boy, do you sleep in the gun-house?"

Allie stood silent.

"Answer!" thundered the doctor, swinging his cane.

"Yes," said Allie.

"Why?"

"To watch the guns, sir."

"Who told you to do that?"

Allie moved back, and a crowd gathered around him.

"Boy, if I find you there to-night, you will know that that cane—do you see it?—that that there cane has Solomon in it."

A deputy came along and stopped before the master.

"Hear ye, Master Holbrooke, hear ye while I read the warrant for the town-meeting, to further discuss the better teaching of Latin and Greek in the schools of the town." The deputy read the warrant for a special town-meeting to continue the discussion of the interesting topic.

Dr. Oliver was a classical scholar, and Sam Adams was a graduate of the Latin School and Harvard University. Sam Adams walked to and fro in a kindly and pleasant way, with his hands behind him.   Dr. Oliver listened impatiently.

"Master Holbrooke," said the doctor, "I am opposed to the teaching of Latin in the town-schools at all.   I believe in educating a few people, and let them, like doctors and lawyers and ministers, instruct the rest.   That is the way it was in King Alfred's day and the times of Charlemagne, when learning flourished.   It makes poor people dissatisfied with their lot to educate them.   Why, Master Holbrooke, only this day one of my patients, just out of the Latin School, had the audacity to ask me what the medicine that I prescribed for him was composed of!   I never was more taken back in my life.   I lifted my cane and reproved him for his impertinence.   And then he, a young man between twenty and thirty, answered me, and said: 'In the progress of education people will come to know what they swallow.'   It was a trifling thing, but it shows the tendency of the times.   When I call a butter-cup a *Ranunculus bulbosa*, it draws a blister, and it wouldn't have the face to if I told the patient just what weed it was.   The education detracts from the dignity of all the learned professions.   I hear that Mrs. Wheatley is teaching black Phillis the dead languages."

"That is why I object to Latin," said the deputy; "because it is a dead language.   No one speaks it now, do they, Master Holbrooke?"

"No; it is the dead language of history, poetry, and

art, and the living language only of the learned professions."

"That's what I tell 'em," said the deputy. "The nations that used to speak that language are all dead now, and if the language had been what it ought to be they wouldn't be dead. We don't want any second-rate, dead things in our schools."

"Very sensibly said," replied Dr. Oliver. "Teach the common people reading, writing, and arithmetic, and if they have any capacity or genius for anything more they can learn it themselves. I'm going to predict, now, if the colonies should unite and form a nation, everybody will have to be educated, else the nation could not last. In such an event my coachman might own a medical dictionary and commit suicide by trying to doctor himself. Learning is the privilege of the few."

"And the right of all," said Master Holbrooke. "I would have every boy and girl in Boston have a classical education."

"You would, would you!" said Dr. Oliver, lifting his cane. "You would have Phillis Wheatley go hand in hand to school with my daughter, and conjugate *amo* together? You'll hear from me next town-meeting day. I'll have my say yet. This is a strange progress of what we call human rights. You believe in such things?"

"Yes Dr. Oliver, I believe in the right of every man to do right when it is consistent with the good of the whole.

J would give to every man his birthright, to every man an equal opportunity, and to all merit its just reward."

"And you would have a scullion read Homer, and if he could do so better than others, you would set him to teach my son?"

"Exactly so," said Master Holbrooke; "exactly so."

"That's what Sam Adams would say, and I do believe that he has converted Hancock to just such views. When that day comes I will quit my country, Master Holbrooke, I'll quit my country. Let me tell you, something is due to blood."

"What?"

"Loyalty."

"The blood that flows in the veins of the Prince of Wales is exactly the same as my own or any other human being's. Royal blood is merely an imagination. How much royal blood has a deposed king?"

"Do you teach such treason as that in your school, Master Holbrooke? The blood of a royal race comes from Heaven-appointed position."

"We will form a nation in which all will be kings. It is in the folkmoot now. England has been governed by men so weak in mind as to be the tools of the worst of men, and so corrupt in morals as to be worthy of no public respect. The town-meeting put the government into the hands of the men of the best brain and character. We will form a nation on that principle."

7

"And let the mob rule. I'll quit my country when that day comes, I will." The doctor swung his cane in the melting air. "I'd.go now if I ever expected to see a day like that. I'll quit my country. You'll hear from me again on next town-meeting day. A few men have had their own way long enough, and now I mean to see what I can do. It is high time that the select few, the saving remnant, regularly appointed, came back to their rightful power."

"And that those few be appointed by the people to do their will, to act merely as representatives."

"Is your school governed in that way, Master Holbrooke?"

"Yes; I am governed by the parents, who support the school."

"How about the scholars?"

"I am influenced by their intelligence and character. It will be so with the new nation. The people who vote must be of an intelligent age and good character."

"It would fail in twenty years."

"Not if it were supported by one thing, Dr. Oliver."

"And what is that?"

"Universal education."

The bell rang. The pupils gathered about the door from the open Common, and waited for the two supervisors, or committeemen, to enter first. Sam Adams, with his animated face, motioned to Dr. Oliver to enter first, and he then followed the exponent of education of the few for the benefit of the many.

Master Holbrooke sat down at the desk, which some scholars had trimmed with evergreens from the Roxbury woods. He called the roll of scholars, each one present answering " Here." He then nicely pointed with his pen-knife a large number of quill pens, and asked the older scholars to write the sentence, *Possunt quia posse videntur*, to sign it, and to hand it to Dr. Oliver and Mr. Adams.

They did so.

" A great improvement," said Mr. Adams, absently. " I read much in these signatures."

" I don't see any improvement," said Dr. Oliver. " This writing is no better than the old black-letter man-uscripts of the days of Thomas à Becket. I used to write better than any of these when I was a boy. My educa-tion was special."

" I mean," said Mr. Adams, " that these signatures are better than those that I have been studying."

" That shows what you have been studying," said Dr. Oliver. " What you mean to say is that these signatures are better than those of the town-meeting clerks, who have been sending you letters of correspondence."

" Yes, my good friend," said Mr. Adams, " that is what was in my mind."

" These boys and girls write well enough for that kind of correspondence," said Dr. Oliver. " It is that kind of correspondence that is making rebels of the whole country, which I expect nothing but I'll have to quit."

Dr. Oliver went over all of the scripts a second time, and he scowled at each. The pupils watched him, some half laughing, others half angry.

Samuel Adams had organized in Boston a Committee of Correspondence. The work of this committee was to correspond with all the towns of the colony concerning what the people regarded as their rights, and how to maintain those rights. The plan grew in popularity and power, and extended to other colonies. In this way Sam Adams gained the sense of the whole people and organized public opinion, and prepared the way for the Revolution.

He was a polished man. He loved to use classical terms and to make classical quotations. He was one of the first of this kind of New England orators, of which Charles Sumner was the last.

He arose to address the school. He spoke in the courteous, eloquent way in which he wrote, and won every heart in the school. Dr. Oliver saw that the man's opinions had come to live or to be crushed.

As Dr. Oliver went out of the school he saw Allie, and raising his cane, said, " Remember!"

Sam Adams's dog Queue came running to meet his master. This dog had so imbibed his master's spirit as to have become, as we have already shown, a terror to Boston redcoats. Two of Dr. Oliver's friends had been attacked by him while engaged in disputes with the Sons of Liberty. The animal had become a source of alarm to redcoats and Tories in lonely ways or in street disputes.

Allie was brave. He had been charged to sleep in the gun-house and to alarm the neighborhood with his drum in case any attempt was made to break into the house at night, and he resolved to go to his post as usual on this night, notwithstanding the doctor's threat.

As he left his home this pleasant spring evening Sam Adams's dog came running toward him, followed by Old Surry. A thought crossed his mind.

"Surry," said he, "let me take the dog along with me to the gun-house to-night."

"Yo' must be lonely dere. Yes, yo' take him 'long wid yo' for company. Massa Adams will not mind. Dese be peaceful times again. Yo're lonely dar, ain't yo', boy? But dar ain't no hants there. De house is new. I thought dat dere war hants dar, but it was jest yo' boys, talkin' about guns, an' hidin' things."

"Come, Queue!"

Allie with his drum turned away toward the gun-house.

He felt a perfect sense of security, for the dog followed him. He and the dog went into the gun-house, and he fastened the door securely, and lay down on a mattress beside the guns, and the great dog lay down beside him.

The nine-o'clock bells rang, and the clocks struck clearly the hour of ten. The town grew silent.

A queer noise began to fall upon Allie's sleeping ear.
It drew nearer.   Steps, and a cane.   Allie listened.   The
dog darted up and was about to growl, when his little
master put his hand over his mouth, and said, " Hush!"

The steps approached, and stopped before the door.
Suddenly Tap, tap, tap, was heard.   It was the noise of
the cane.

The dog attempted to leap forward, but Allie held him
back and kept his hand over his mouth.   The animal
seemed to understand that he was to keep silent and wait.

Tap, tap, tap!

" Who is there? "

" You open this door and you'll find who is here."

Rap, rap, rap!

" Do you hear that, boy?   You open this door."

" What right have you to demand that I should open
the door?   I was told to watch the guns."

" The right of being your superior, boy."

" But you are not the superior of the Sons of Liberty,
who have given me this charge.   The guns belong to the
citizens of Boston, and I am charged to guard them."

" And what would you do if the authorities had come
to take them? "

" I would beat my drum and arouse the Sons."

" Well, beat your drum and arouse the Sons, but first
do you open this door."

Rap, rap, rap!

The dog uttered a low growl, followed by a piercing howl.

" Great Cæsar!" exclaimed the doctor; "is that Queue? You—you—needn't open the door. I only called around to see if you wanted anything."

Allie heard rapidly retreating steps. He looked out of the window, and saw the doctor hastily plodding past the Frog Pond. Then the night fell still.

CHAPTER IX.

THE PATRIOT SCHOOL.

O, seize and put under guard all the guns and ammunition belonging to the town!" Such was in substance the order of General Gage. It reached the ears of some patriots and flew through the town.

Where were the seven boys and young men who had pledged themselves to guard the cannon in the gun-house? They had need of action now.

Two of the four guns were being used by the Sons of Liberty outside of the gun-house. An order came that these should be detained in view of the public training-ground where the king's troops were quartered.

The seven boys met. Two of the cannon were already under guard; how could they secure the other two in the gun-house and conceal them?

The boys met under the mighty tent of the old elm tree. They had learned the master's proverb that in publicity is the best hiding-place. Their meeting was held in full view of the king's officers. They consulted, then sent for the patriot schoolmaster.

" I would remove the guns now, in open day," he said. " I would hide them in the wood-box of our own school-room. Boys, listen: it is my view that if we can hide those guns and secure the other two, we can one day compel the British troops to evacuate Boston. Think what those guns could do on Roxbury Hill or Milton Hill or Dorchester Heights! Sam Adams says that the town must have those four guns, and Sam Adams is a prophet."

" We have pledged our honor to the guns," said Philip Fayreweather.

" There is no time to be lost," said the patriot school-master.

" What shall be done?" asked all.

The schoolmaster looked around, and viewed the situation. There, in full view of the sentinels and guards, stood the gun-house with open doors. It was high noon.

"Allie, rattle your drum and summon the boys to a game of tag. Let the boys from time to time rush by the gun-house in a body. Do you see what I mean? Let the rest of you secure the aid of some stout men, Sons of Liberty. When the boys run past the door of the gun-house, at some favorable moment, rushing, tumbling, screaming, roll the guns behind them out of the gun-house into the schoolhouse. I will be there. This may be a day of destiny if we succeed. If the guns are secured they will speak for liberty some day—who can tell!"

Ten minutes later the roll of Allie's drum called nearly a hundred boys to the playground. A wild, rollicking game of tag was begun, and the master watched it from the door. It lasted long, and the boys circled around the Frog Pond again and again. The British officers watched them. The excitement grew. Once, when the whole crowd seemed to be tumbling over each other at a point between the gun-house and the training-grounds, the schoolmaster disappeared and the door of the schoolhouse suddenly closed.

All was animation as the boys leaped up and circled the Frog Pond again. Suddenly the sentinel near the gun-house blew a whistle. He then stood as one transfixed. The guard came hurrying toward him.

" Look there!" he said, with a gasp.

" What? " asked the guard.

" The guns in the gun-house."

" There are none there."

" No—and we are responsible. They were there."

The sentinel strode like a wild man to the officers' tent. The school-bell rang.

Among the leaders in this most remarkable transaction was James Brewer, who Drake in his " Boston Tea Party " biographies informs us was one of the young men " who removed at *noonday*, and while it was yet under guard, the [brace of] cannon from the gun-house on West Street."

A company of redcoats came marching down to West Street, and passed the door of the writing-school. The school was now in session, and the master seemed to be absorbed in his duties.

" Halt!" said the captain.

The red-coated men stopped, and an orderly opened the gun-house door.

" Advance!"

The men advanced and entered the gun-house.

They needed no order to halt. The captain stopped, and uttered a profane exclamation; the men stared about on four empty gun-carriages and empty space.

" Where are the guns?" cried the captain, stamping. The hollow sound of his own voice was his only answer.

" Those lawless boys!" he exclaimed. " Break rank! Search every house on the street. I will search the school-house."

The captain with a commanding step entered the school-house. Master Holbrooke had begun to put aside the regular profession of teaching, but he was that day at his post.

" Holbrooke, I have but few words to say—the guns are gone, and you know where they are. Tell me at once, or I will order your arrest."

In the schoolroom there were more than a hundred

pupils, most of them boys of from thirteen to nineteen years of age. The room was as still as death when the captain entered. Master Holbrooke stood at his desk, book in hand, and a quill pen behind his ear. He looked down on the officer calmly, and said :

" To whom are you speaking, sir? "

" To you, sir."

" I am not accustomed to have my room entered in this way, or to be addressed in any such manner as this. What is your business, sir? "

" The cannon have been stolen from the gun-house right under your very eyes. You or your scholars must know where they went. It is my business to search the house. Have you a ladder to the scuttle? "

" Philip Fayreweather, hang the ladder that leads to the scuttle."

The ladder was brought. The officer made an awkward figure in climbing to the dark pyramidal chamber of the roof.

" Shut him up there!" whispered several of the boys. Master Holbrooke raised his hand warningly, and there followed a deep silence.

As the officer descended he was offered a chair by the master, which was placed as close as possible to the great wooden box that contained the seasoned fuel for the fire.

" Master Holbrooke, cannon do not fly about in the air,

nor run about on the ground. There is but one thing that carries away cannon, and that is legs; and four cannon never disappear from a place like this without their going being seen by somebody. I want to call every boy here before me and question him."

" You are at liberty to do so, though I doubt your right to do so. Those cannon belong to our own townspeople, do they not?"

" They belong to the defenders of his Majesty's colony. Let each boy be called."

" There is the register, sir. Call the names yourself."

" You will compel them to answer, sir?"

" No, sir; I shall leave it to each boy to answer you as he pleases. This is not a matter that belongs to the school."

" What! do you mean to tell me that right and royal government is not a matter that belongs to this school?"

The officer opened the register.

" Let me make a warmer fire," said the master. He opened the wood-box, and took from it some heavy, hard sticks, uncovering the pile of wood before the officer's eyes as he did so. He did not replace the cover on the box. When the fire was well rekindled he threw the shovel on the wood, and asked the captain for his hat, which he placed on the box. He then leaned against the box.

The officer began to call the boys. He asked each

boy: "Do you know where the cannon that were in the gun-house are?"

Fifty boys had answered, "No, sir, I do not."

"Philip Fayreweather."

The young man arose.

"Philip Fayreweather, do you know where the cannon that were in the gun-house now are?"

The crisis had come. Our little drummer-boy saw it; there flashed across his mind a way to solve his brother's difficulty. He knew that Philip would not lie or equivocate, and that he would never tell what he must have known.

He raised his hand.

"Master Holbrooke, may I go home?"

The master saw, and every boy who knew where the cannon had been saw also a way of escape from the trying position in which they were placed. "You may be excused," said the master.

The officer saw how shrewdly the boy had opened a way of escape for any who should be unwilling to answer his questions.

"You drum?" said the officer to the little lad, as he prepared to go.

"Yes."

"You are Sam Adams's little drummer, are you not? Say, little boy, have you not learned that there is none greater than the king?"

"No, sir; the master never taught me that."

"Who is greater than the king, my lad?"

"They who take the crown from the king—the people."

"You little rebel! in your eyes Sam Adams and his followers are greater than King George. Don't you know that the king has arms like the lion and the unicorn?"

"There are no lions in this country, and Master Holbrooke says that there are no unicorns anywhere."

"You'll find out what those figures mean before long," said the officer. "Master Holbrooke, this is a school of treason. It was some of these boys who went to General Gage and demanded of him the protection of their snow-forts on the Common. The general saw what little rebels they were. The very air of this town is full of treason, and this school ought to be closed."

He gazed with a heavy frown on the school, which began to wear a very animated expression.

Philip still stood silent.

"Philip Fayreweather, answer me. I am an officer of the crown. Do you know where those cannon are?"

The boy stood silent as before.

"Philip Fayreweather, answer!"

The room was still. The red sun was going down; there was a fiery splendor behind the great gray shadows of the South End elms. A cold breeze rattled the windows. But beyond these expressions of nature there was neither motion nor sound.

The officer leaped up with an angry glow in his face.

" Master Holbrooke, command that boy to answer."

" Philip," said the master, "you may answer as you choose."

" Master Holbrooke," said Philip, in a firm voice.

" Well, Philip ? "

" May I come to the wood-box ? "

" Yes."

Two other boys made the same request.

The officer looked alarmed. Were these boys about to attack him from the wood-box?

The three boys had somehow made a secret communication with one. another. They approached the box, opened the top more widely than before, and took from the box not missiles with which to attack the officer, but their caps and satchels.

" Master Holbrooke," said Philip Fayreweather, " may we be excused ? "

" You may be excused," said the master. " The whole school is dismissed."

The boys rushed toward the great wood-box, where their caps and winter coverings had been placed. The officer looked suspiciously at the box, so full of weapons that might be raised by these young, unfriendly hands, and moved toward the door. He did not dream that more dangerous weapons were in that very box, and that he would hear their voice one day.

And, strange to tell, Master Holbrooke, who had a lame or gouty foot, sat down near this same box, and raising the disabled foot, put it upon the box. Of all the objects in the room the wood-box was the least likely to fall under the officer's suspicions. And it did not so fall. The simple act was an event in the history of the country, which we must here better understand.

General Gage had succeeded Governor Hutchinson, and had come back to Boston with a strong military force. Governor Hutchinson, who had been born in Boston and educated at Harvard, went to England, leaving behind his beautiful home on Milton Hill. He was a favorite of the court, but he loved New England, and he once said: " I would rather die in a New England country-house than in any castle in the best nobleman's seat in England!" His beautiful estate on Milton Hill, not far from the house of the " Suffolk Resolves," may still be seen.

The General Court, or Massachusetts Assembly, met in 1774 at Salem. Samuel Adams, through his Committees of Correspondence, had prepared the delegates to elect representatives to a Provincial Congress of the colonies. But Gage must not know of this. Were the governor to suspect such a movement he would dissolve the assembly.

So when the assembly met, Sam Adams locked the door and put the key in his pocket. But one of the delegates, who was a Tory, feigned sickness, and was allowed to leave the room, and he hastened to Boston to inform Gen-

. 8

eral Gage of what was going on at Salem.   The governor
sent a deputy to prorogue the assembly.   But Sam Adams
still had the key of the room in his own pocket, and he
would not allow the deputy to enter until the delegates to
the new congress had been elected.   Of these delegates
he himself was one.   When the door was unlocked the
assembly was already dissolved.

   This was sharp practice indeed for the so-called "last
of the Puritans," and the foremost man of the Christian
Sparta.   But in all history there are to be found few more
unselfish men than the same Sam Adams.   He sought
nothing for himself, but everything for the cause.   He
never sought office for fame, and he died poor.   He was
a cause: himself, nothing.   The humbler people of Boston
looked upon him as a prophet.   He seemed like one who
had forgotten himself; yet he was always at the head of
the cause.   Except Washington, he was the most illustrious of Americans.

   Such was the political field at this time.

   The schoolmaster bade the boys leave the building after
the school was dismissed, though he held a secret conference with a few of them before they went away.

   For a time he sat alone on this mellow September
evening.

   As the sunset faded among the tree-tops of the Common, a firm step approached, and Sam Adams opened the
door.

" Here ? " he said, bowing courteously.

" Yes ; on guard."

" You have won a battle without a shot," said the man of the town-meeting. " It is not often that one catches so many cannon by his wits alone."

" Mr. Adams, do you comprehend what this means? The school has won a battle in a contest with the crown. The guns are in that box, and this lame foot saved them in the end."

" And won a notable victory. The guns are silent now, but mark my words, they will one day be needed. You will hear them speak. But what is to be done with them ? "

" They will be taken to-night to some hiding-place."

" How, my good friend ? "

" In some hay-carts or coal-carts. The secret is intrusted to Blingo."

" I have no fears for their safety, if that be the case. Blingo has a true heart, quick wit, and a firm hand. He is a host in himself."

" Mr. Adams, these are serious times; the country is arming, and what is to be the end ? "

" Liberty ! "

" At the cost of blood ? "

" Yes, at the cost of blood ! "

" And the guns in that wood-box may lead the way."

" Yes, they may mow the earth."

"Mr. Adams, do you know that a price is set upon
your own head?"

"I do not count myself if the cause may only prevail.
I may be sent into exile; I may be executed or fall in an
affray. The pilot of the 'Argo' may not return, but the
'Argo' of Liberty will return, and bring the *Golden
Fleece!*"

"The new cause of mankind is at hand. It means liberty for the nation, and if for this nation, why not for all
nations? In fancy I can almost hear those field-pieces
thunder. But a new cause only advances through the
blood of those who hold the cause of justice to all men as
dearer than life."

"My friend, the crisis is upon us. Listen: I would
have the cause go forward, even if it were revealed to me
from heaven that nine hundred out of every thousand
men in our nation were to fall. The remnant would be
nobler than a thousand slaves. If such were to refound
the nation in liberty and justice, it would repay the sacri-
fice. I expect nothing for myself—I want nothing. I
have made my peace with the King of kings, and I have
offered my all to mankind."

The schoolmaster arose, his lame foot still resting on
the wood-box.

"All that I am I give to this cause. Human liberty
waits to lift mankind to a higher destiny. May these
cannon, if needed, lead the way to days of human glory,

when men shall receive their birthright, and elect and dis-
pose of their own rulers, or the representatives who shall
execute their own will."

"Glorious!" said the statesman. "My friend, you express it well. What your words picture I see."

He stood bowed.

"We shall struggle," he said, "and we shall win. But
I shall not share in the glory."

There was heard the rattle of Allie's drum in the yard.
It was filling the silent chambers of the air with that
lively tune which had floated from the Castle when the
two regiments came.

"I may not share in the glory," he added, "but I shall
be content if one day such boys as those may follow me
in the streets and say that I helped to make a nation for
the schools. For if we have a nation founded on the
principles of the town-meeting, its only hope will be in the
schools."

"That would be a glorious day, indeed, when a free
people should put their trust in the schoolhouse rather
than in the fortress," said the patriot schoolmaster.

Night came, but the master remained on guard. The
next morning when the school gathered the great wood-
box was empty, except of some kindlings and a store of
wood.

CHAPTER X.

AMUEL ADAMS had a principle in politics something like this: " Put your enemy on the wrong side in public opinion and keep him there until he yields," or, in other words, " Make the gravitation of wrong to be seen to be wrong." The patriot schoolmaster had a like maxim: " Silence is the voice that wins;" and when he appeared before his school on the following morning he merely said:

"You have been told how the 'Gaspee' insulted our ships in Narragansett Bay, and compelled them to lower their flags to her. A smart craft, drawing but little water, afterward allured her to follow in her course, and caused her to run aground. A party of men from Providence went down to the stranded ship at night and burned her. She will cause no more ships to haul down their flags to her. There must have been from fifty to a hundred men in the party that boarded and burned the 'Gaspee.' A fortune in gold was offered for the arrest of the leaders of those men. A High Court of Inquiry was held at Newport. A long time has passed since that helpless ship lay rolling in fire on the shoals of the bay ; but, my boys, has any one been able to find any proof against one of those men? No. That is patriotic silence. There have been such silences in history. He who breaks such a silence is a traitor, a coward, or a fool. I have no such boys in my school. *Silence !* You may take your books. *Silence!* "

It was a still school. Nothing had been said or advised in regard to the present situation, but the soul of the master's words was in the air. There would be silence.

There was a smithy and a red forge under some great trees at the North End, not far from the place where lived Paul Revere, and just off of the " fair greene lan' of Boston town." The smithy was known as " Blingo's, the black-smith." The cool sea-winds blew its fires, which in turn illumined the sea at night where now lie the naval ships.

Blingo was an illiterate, stalwart man. His muscles were hardened by swinging the hammer, and his hair was white and his beard gray. He was a very superstitious man, and the neighborhood where he lived abounded with the fearful witch tales of Cotton Mather's day. His shop for thirty years had been a place of resort for story-tell-ing loungers. Blingo had learned from many sources the terrible legends of Mercy Short and Margaret Rule, of the witchcraft days, and he used to relate them with all the vivid colorings and accretions of many witnesses.

The Old North Church lifted its spire over the hill under which the smithy stood. In it was and still is a famous chime of bells.

There was another maxim which the patriot school-master used to repeat in those times of secrecy : "Always hide a thing in the most conspicuous place, for that is the last place that is likely to be searched."

At the beginning of the watching of the four guns the smithy of Blingo had been thought of as a hiding-place, and now that a place must be found for two of them, and as they could not well be taken over the water or across the guarded Boston Neck, the master began to think again of his own motto, and the thronged shop of Blingo, the blacksmith.

The original guard of seven had grown in years and in numbers since the meetings in the gun-house which had so terrified Old Surry. The party now called themselves "The Younger Sons of Liberty," and little Allie and his drum had been admitted to it. In this way he obtained his appointment as a night-watch. A larger society was at last formed in the same spirit, called "The Incorrupt-ible Thirty."

That night after the stratagem and the search of the schoolhouse a meeting had been called by the master to determine where the guns should be placed for security, and Blingo the blacksmith had been invited to meet the boys and young men who had sworn to protect the guns.

The boys met at the foot of the Liberty Tree, close by the schoolhouse. The master addressed them briefly:

" I will not counsel silence : it would wound your honor. Any of you would rather die than be an informer.

" You are all asking me in your minds what shall be done with the two guns. I would trust them to Blingo." And he whispered to Philip: " I would hide them in the coal-bins of Blingo the blacksmith, where all the people can see the coal.

" Blingo, can we trust you with the guns? We do not wish to know anything more. You have bins and stables, and live down by the sea."

" Aye, a wise master that you are. Blingo will protect the guns with his life. Aye, you may trust me for that, and if any one comes around silent-like, any laced Tory or Britisher, I will tell him the story of the haunted chamber of Mercy Short or of Margaret Rule, and he will see things in the air. The redcoats shall never see those guns again until they hear them."

" Or of ' the window in the forest,' " said the master. " One must have nerves to look about much in dark places after such a story as that."

" The window in the forest " was one of Blingo's many-times-told tales.

" And how shall the guns be taken to Blingo? " asked Philip Fayreweather.

" You may trust me for that," said Blingo.

"I move that we make Blingo a committee of one for
the removal of the guns," said the master; "that we trust
everything to him, and so have as few as possible in the
secret."

The motion was assented to.   Boston was now a town
of mysteries.   People were everywhere talking about their
"charter rights" and the "redress of their grievances."
But Sam Adams, all alone in teaching this simple community their grand opportunity, was dreaming of the union
of the American colonies as an independent nation.   The
fulfilment of that lonely·dream is America.   I know of
few lessons more inspiring than this picture of the self-
forgetful patriot thus walking in his lonely reveries the
streets of Boston town.

CHAPTER XI.

THE disappearance of the guns from the gun-house, and the failure of the British officers to find them, was the mystery of the town. Some said the guns had been sent to Concord, some to Worcester, but many people believed that they were still hidden in the place.

The two other cannon were placed on the Common, near where the Park Street gate now is, and were kept under guard.

But now a more mysterious thing happened in open day. While the British soldiers were off duty, and the sentinel who had been charged to watch the guns was pacing to and fro, a young man was seen hurrying toward the place in a determined and excited way. He faced the sentinel, and raising a pistol, said:

" Do you see that? "

The sentinel, with his back to the guns, gazed in terror at the weapon which was levelled before his eyes.

" What does this mean? " asked the sentinel.

" It means that I have you in my power, and that our townsmen have sent me to relieve you of your duty. We are tired of seeing your red coat passing to and fro on our Common and guarding the guns which belong to us for our own defence."

The sentinel attempted to look around. The young man lifted the hammer of the lock.

" Redcoat, don't you stir. If you do, you will answer for the consequences. Did you know that this town is full of clubs? Have you heard of the club that meets at the Green Dragon? Do you know of the Incorruptible Thirty, whose leader is Paul Revere? Even the school has clubs."

" Sir, what does this mean?" faltered the sentinel. " What brings you here? Don't you know that you will be arrested for hindering a British soldier in the discharge of his duty?"

" No, I will not be arrested."

" Why? On account of the strength of the clubs? You are under orders, so am I. I am ordered to guard the guns. If you do not like it, why do you not go to tl · superior officers?"

" I am ordered to relieve you of your duty. I am going to count one hundred, and while I do so I want that you should look directly at the muzzle of this pistol. If you stir it will flash fire; when I have counted one hundred I

Disappearance of "guarded" cannon.

shall give you my order. Are you ready? One—two
—three. Silence!"

There were gatherings of people behind the sentinel,
and a hurried passing to and fro, but the sentinel did not
dare to look around.

The young man continued to count slowly, with his
hand on the lock.

"One hundred," said he at last. "Now for my order.
I will drop my pistol at my side, and you may look
around. This is all a joke."

The sentinel turned, and looked toward the place where
the guns had been stationed for him to guard. There
was nothing there. A joke, indeed! Could he believe
his eyes! No guns, no soldiers, nothing but calm sunshine and empty air. A few people were gathered across
the street near where Winter Street now opens its crowded
way to Washington Street.

The sentinel's eyes protruded, and then turned in wild
astonishment toward the young patriot.

"Who has done this?"

"The witches!" *

The sentinel looked into the air, where the witches were
supposed to fly, but he saw no guns.

---

* " The Whigs first carried off two of the cannon, and though the other
two were put under guard they carried them off also. This made the officers
mad. They said that they believed the devil got them away."—FROTHING-
HAM's " Siege of Boston."

A company of British soldiers were approaching. The
young man moved rapidly back, and soon was lost to
view in the street behind the hill where the Soldiers'
Monument now stands, and which at that day overlooked
the marshes, for such then was the place where the beautiful Public Garden and lower Beacon Street now are.

The news of the loss of the cannon was carried to the
Province House, where General Gage was, and astonished
the British soldiers and spread through the town. Soldiers
hurried to and fro searching for the guns; Boston Neck
was guarded and the ferries were watched. But the guns
were never seen again in the streets of Boston unless it
may be on that day of triumph which we shall try to por-
tray in our last chapter. But they were *heard* there.

Among those who went in search of the guns was busy
Dr. Oliver with his cane.

"It is an outrage!" he said to every one; "and I'll
quit my country if such things go on."

The haunted blacksmith's shop of Blingo was always
a popular place of resort. As young people had always
liked to go there and listen to the dark blacksmith's
strange stories, it was not strange that they should go
there now. The witch stories of Cotton Mather's day
lasted for a generation, and Cotton Mather himself slept
near the shop on Copp's Hill. The wind of the sea waved
the great trees mysteriously over the sloping graveyard.
The waves dashed at the foot of the hill after the storms.

After the disappearance of the guns the benches under the great trees in front of the smithy became filled with young men on pleasant nights. The shop doors stood open, and the great forge blazed after every movement of the bellows. The Sons of Liberty liked to go there to talk, as well as to the Liberty Tree. The West School boys found the place more than interesting, as the reader may surmise. Paul Revere, the leading spirit of the Incorruptible Thirty, lived near the place.

It was upon this place that Dr. Oliver began to look with suspicion.

One night he went down there to enjoy the spell-like atmosphere, and to see if he could find a single point to confirm his suspicions that Blingo and a part of his young visitors were in the secret of the concealment of the guns.

The open ground in front of the smithy was full of young people, mostly boys, with a few older men. Allie was there with his drum, and Queue sat like a giant by his side. The dog growled as the doctor approached, but Allie clasped him by the neck.

"A fine evening, my young friends," said the doctor. "What is it that brings so many of you here to-night?"

The blacksmith, with a red-hot iron bar in his tongs, looked out of the door. His face was black with soot, which gave his eyes a peculiarly white appearance, and he presented a weird figure in the light of the blazing forge.

Dr. Oliver walked into the shop. He began to poke his cane into the soft coal of the bins. When the fire deadened, leaving the place dark, he would lift the lever of the bellows, and all would grow light again.

In punching the soft coal in the bins with his cane he came to something hard.

" I do believe that's those guns," said he, punching away.

The young men started up and ran into the shop, and a few of them seemed excited.

" Boys," said the doctor, " you just lift the coal out of that bin, and I'll blow."

The doctor seized the lever of the bellows and blew until a high fire filled all of the shop with light.

Some of the boys began to handle the coal.

" That's right," said the doctor, " lift it out."

" Then you must put it back again," said the black-smith.

The boys hesitated. There were two young men whom the doctor well knew, and he commanded them to lift the coal out of the bin.

" I will see that it is put back again," said he to Blingo.

The blacksmith stood silent. Three of the young men approached him. The doctor blew the fire, while the coal was being slowly removed from the bin.

The doctor became nervous, and blew the fire so act-ively that the charcoal rushed up in a high stream of flame.

"That will never do," said the blacksmith; "do you mean to burn my shop?"

He seized a bucket of water and dashed it on to the flames, then another and another. There arose a steamy smoke which filled the shop with darkness, and all the inmates rushed out-of-doors.

CHAPTER XII.

HE disappearance of the four guns filled Boston town with lively curiosity. Where had they gone? Boston Neck was guarded by British troops, so they could not have passed out of the town openly in that way. The sentinel declared that the "devil" carried away the two which he was guarding, and the British soldiers wondered if the days of witchcraft were indeed gone.

" There is one person who knows where they are," said the pompous old Tory, Dr. Oliver, " and that is that little drummer-boy, Allie Fayreweather."

Dr. Oliver met Allie on the Common the next day. He bent his eyes on him loftily and suspiciously, and said:

" Boy, come here. I want to talk with you."

Allie stopped.

" What do you do when you meet your elders and superiors ? "

" I treat them as well as I can, sir."

116

" Treat them well? You take off your hat, don't you, like a gentleman? "

" Yes, sir," said Allie, and he uncovered his head.

" That is right. And what do you do when your elders and superiors ask you questions? "

" I answer them, sir, as well as I can, sir."

" You speak the truth? "

" Always, sir."

" Now look me right in the eye. Allie Fayreweather, do you know where the two guns are that were in the gun-house? "

" I do not, sir."

" Do you know of any one who helped hide them or carry them away? "

" I cannot answer you, sir."

" Cannot! Why? You seem to have a loose tongue. Now, boy, I am your elder and superior, and I demand that you answer that question. Do you know any of the persons who hid those guns? "

" If I did, I could not give you their names, sir."

" A boy has no right with a secret."

" A boy has no right to break promises, sir."

" A boy has no right to make a promise."

" I think that he has, with his parents' permission. I have no secret that I would not be willing that my mother should know, sir, and I do nothing in school that I would be unwilling that my mother should know."

"Does your mother know who stole and hid those guns?"

"I think that she does not."

"Boy, this transaction took place in school hours—at the noon recess. Now the master is responsible for the scholars; he is their superior. But I am a trustee, boy. I am his superior, and you are bound, out of regard to the rightful authority, to tell me who stole and hid those cannon."

"I wish to do just what is right, sir, but I must talk first with my mother and then with the master, and then with those to whom I have made promises."

"Boy, you shall talk with no one. I am town authority in school matters, and there is none higher than I. Now, right here, without any further delay, tell me, do you know of any one who helped to carry away those guns?"

"Dr. Oliver, is it ever right for a boy to break his word?"

"Your question is impertinent. You have treated me disrespectfully, and I will punish you, if it costs me a suit at law with Sam Adams. Boy, come here."

"Spare me, sir. I meant no disrespect. I am only trying to do what is right."

"Take off your jacket, boy. I would not destroy a widow's spinning and weaving. *That* cane hits hard." The doctor lifted his cane and looked up at it significantly.

"Let me speak to Mr. *Adams*, sir. I will do anything that he tells me. He is my elder and superior."

"You little sauce-box!" The doctor stared.

"And he is a trustee, too, sir."

"Did I ever hear the equal of that for impertinence! Here, where are you going?"

"To the school, sir."

"Well, I will be after you. Go right along. You'll rue the day when you dared to answer back to me."

Allie went to the schoolhouse, and sat two hours in terror, expecting that Dr. Oliver would appear.

Just as the school was about to close the trustee came.

"Master Holbrooke," said he, "I hope I find you well. I've called on a very peculiar errand. Is that drummer-boy here?"

"Allie Fayreweather?"

"Yes, sir."

"I wish you would ask him to step out here a moment. I wish to speak with him."

Allie was sent to the door. He responded, trembling. Dr. Oliver laid his hand on his arm, and drew him out into the yard. He tightened his grasp, and said:

"Now, you little rebel, I am going to make an example of you, and a spectacle to all the school and people."

The doctor lifted his cane.

There was a loud warning bark at the end of the street. The doctor dropped Allie's arm and turned nervously.

He saw Old Surry coming toward the place, and Queue was with her. The dog had seen the raised cane.

"What will you do if I let you go?" said Dr. Oliver.

"Right, sir."

"And always speak the truth?"

"Always, sir."

"Well, I'll have to let you off this time, seeing that Sam Adams is the other trustee and a man in authority like myself, and I have not consulted yet with him."

The scholars came bounding out of the door. Their many voices rang over the playground. Dr. Oliver was not pleased with the merriment, and he frowned in a way that cast a shadow, a thing in marked contrast with Sam Adams's pleasant face, which caused young faces to light and glow wherever he went. The children of Boston used to follow Adams about the streets in his old age, and they had a like affection for him now.

Dr. Oliver glanced once more at Queue. The dog was running toward him, and the doctor hastily entered the house, and there sat down to talk with the patriot school-master.

"Are you sure," said he, "that this house has been thoroughly searched?" The doctor looked toward the scuttle-room under the roof.

"Quite so, sir."

"You are sure that those guns are not hidden some-where up under the roof?"

" Quite so, sir. The attic has been searched."

Dr. Oliver looked toward the ladder that led to the scuttle-room.

" It would have been rather hard work to take them up there. But it looks to me that it would be just the place a rebel would have taken them."

" They are not there."

" Then where are they? They didn't fly away. Nobody has seen any guns in the sky, though the British sentinel thinks that the other two went that way. They didn't sink into the earth. They may be under the floor. Now this is dastardly business. I am determined to have a thorough search, and I will find those guns, and when I do, somebody will have to suffer. I would not spare my own son in a case like that. I would not spare you if you were guilty."

Dr. Oliver looked again at the ladder which led to the roof-room.

" I am heavier than I used to be. Is that ladder safe? "

" It has oak rounds, sir."

" Then I declare, as old as I am, I am going up *there!* "

The doctor went up the ladder toward the dark peaked attic very carefully. He drew his heavy form up into the dusty cavern, and stepped from beam to beam.

Just then the door of the schoolroom opened, and Queue came barking in. The doctor turned from the dusty distance from the scuttle, and came back to the top of the ladder and looked down.

The dog saw him, and became furious. He ran to the foot of the ladder, growling and howling, and in the silences showing his teeth.

The doctor bent over the scuttle-way, and looked down, shaking his cane at the dog.

" Call him away," said he to the master.

" Queue," said the master, " here—come here."

But the dog did not obey.

The doctor now shook his head at Queue. In doing so his wig dropped off, and the dog seized it, and putting his paw upon it, looked up with a savage howl at the doctor.

" What are you going to do now? " said the doctor.

" Call that black woman, Surry."

" She has gone."

" Gone! " muttered the doctor. His face turned white. " Send for Sam Adams, and tell him I will prosecute him for disturbing the peace. I wish that I had a gun!"

" I'll have to send for Allie."

" Well! this is an awful position to be in. There are some things in this world which are maddening. Send for the boy, and tell him that I will forgive him. This is no place for a man in my position to be. Do go, quick!"

The master called Allie, and when the dog had followed

him out of the door the doctor slowly descended, and he did not stop to examine the floor, but hastily sought the cool Common.

" It is no wonder," he said, " that the British think the Evil One is in the place. I'll quit my country. The town is full of rebels, and Sam Adams is the arch-leader of them all.

" But," he added, " I have a suspicion, and the more I think of it the more I think that it is a true one. The two guns are in the blacksmith's shop. Blingo knows where they are. I'll go back again to the smithy, and I will take an officer with me, and Blingo shall tell all that he knows or I will have him arrested."

The doctor paced to and fro under the great trees of the Common. From time to time he lifted his cane, saying :

˙ " I'll have him arrested. The devil won't fly away with any guns when I get my eyes upon them, one may be sure of that—one may be sure of that. I'll have him arrested. I'll go there this very night, and there won't be any fooling when I put my foot down firm."

The doctor stopped and stamped. The lights were being lighted in the British officers' tent on the Common, and he turned and went there to relate his suspicions, and to ask for a posse to go with him to Blingo's, saying, as he went along :

" I'll have him arrested!" and adding at last, " If I find

them out I'll have them all arrested, or I'll quit, quit, quit
my country! They may fool a shaky sentinel, but they
will never fool old Dr. Oliver. Anvils don't fly through
the sky; nor cannon. I'll have him arrested! I'll have
them all arrested! I'll have the schoolmaster arrested, the
boys and all! "

CHAPTER XIII.

THE blacksmith was very busy the next day, so much so that his doors, which usually stood open to the sun, were for several hours closed and fastened. Philip Fayreweather spent the morning with him, and while the doors were closed Philip was with him, and the 'prentice-boy was sent to watch outside, and to report if any one was seen coming. Queue was also there.

The Indian summer afternoon burned on the hills, the sun crisping the leaves for the sea winds to scatter when the calm should be broken. Men came with oxen to be shod; men whose horses had cast shoes, and men to talk over the mysteries of the times.

At the cool nightfall an old stage-driver came. He used to drive the stage from the Boston Stone (still to be seen just off of Hanover Street) and the Green Dragon Inn to the cape towns and Plymouth. He had left the route in middle age to drive an Albany mail-coach to New York. He was an old man now. His name was Cameron.

There was a large gathering of young men about the smithy in the early evening. Paul Revere came over from his foundry, and led for a time the discussion in regard to the four cannon. Every one believed that Paul Revere knew just where the four guns were. It was also believed that Blingo knew, and that a few of the young men were in the secret that two of the guns had been intrusted to the blacksmith's care.

In the midst of the talk Blingo appeared at the door of the smithy.

" Blingo," said Paul Revere, " they say that you have fallen under the suspicion of the British officers. What would you do if they should send to arrest you ? "

" I will never be arrested alive," said the blacksmith. " Trust my wits, Paul Revere ; you and your Incorruptible Thirty are not the only men who have virtue and vigilance in this town. I may be a blacksmith, but you will find me true, and equal to what happens. You wait and see. I was not brought up in the woods to be scared at an owl. You do your work, and I will do mine!"

" Blingo, there is one man whom we must all meet with still tongues. That is Dr. Oliver, who is always about ' to quit his country.' "

Just as Paul Revere had spoken one of the young men said, " Look there! He is coming now."

Dr. Oliver was coming, with his big wig and cane.

Revere walked away, saying, " It is time to change the subject. Blingo, tell a story."

" I am in no frame of mind to tell a story to-night," said Blingo. " Cameron, tell us one of your adventures on the stage."

Dr. Oliver joined the company and sat down with them under the trees.

" I thought that I would just come over the hill, boys, to hear what you had got to say. These are stirring times, and one likes to keep one's eyes and ears open, because none of us know what's going to happen. It's a fine evening."

No one answered.

" A fine evening, so it is. What makes you all so silent ? No intrusion, I hope?"

" Cameron was about to tell us a story," said Philip Fayreweather. " We had just asked him to do so."

" Well, don't let me hinder you. I hoped that you had some theory to offer about those guns. Two of them seem to have sunk into the earth, and the other two to have flown away. I would like to discuss that subject with you. It is on everybody's mind now; but we'll talk of that by and by. Go on with your story-telling."

The assembly under the trees increased. Men from the clubs came quietly over the hill, nodded, and sat down in silence.

At last came Allie and Queue.

"Brought your dog with you," said Dr. Oliver to Allie.
"That dog ain't fit to run loose; he ought to be chained.
So had his master, it is my opinion," the doctor added in
a low voice. He alluded to Sam Adams, and the remark
was listened to in dead silence.

The blacksmith looked out of the shop. His face was
black as soot, and he wore a large leather apron, and his
shirt-sleeves were rolled back almost to his elbow.

"Now, Cameron," he said.

Allie and Queue sat down beside the old stage-driver.
The boy and the dog both knew him well.

"That dog reminds me," said Cameron, "of one that I
used to own. My dog was ready for any emergency, and
I imagine that this one would be, if one were to come."

Dr. Oliver looked at Queue.

"Boy," he said to Allie, "you had better take that dog
home when Cameron has told his story. You and that
dog ought not to be out nights. Mr. Adams ought to
keep his dog at home, and your mother ought to keep
you there. That dog attacked me once, and it is a shame
that I cannot sit down under the trees to listen to a story
without being disturbed by a dangerous animal which has
injured a half-dozen of the king's soldiers while doing
their duty. I sometimes think that I will have to quit
my country."

The doctor looked far away over the harbor, and Cameron began his very curious story:

"These are very mysterious times." Cameron looked at Dr. Oliver. "Cannon fly away just like birds, or run like woodchucks into the ground. The story which I will tell you comes up before me, and seems to fit the place. What shall I call it?

"There lived in Boston, in Governor Belcher's day, or some thirty or more years before those stirring times, a usurer who was known as Tom Walker. In those days of superstition there were people who believed that a man might sell his soul to the Evil One and receive in return the wisdom to become cunning, rich, and powerful. Tom Walker was believed to have sold his soul. He was hated by every one to whom he loaned money in those hard times, and he became very rich; and he disappeared suddenly, and, according to the old story, in a very fearful way."

Now the story which was current that two of the guns had been carried off by witchcraft suggested the story of Tom Walker to the stage-driver. He wished to make the doctor nervous, for he instinctively believed him to be a spy.

"I will tell you the story of Tom Walker," said the stage-driver. "The guns may have gone after him."

"Great Ajax!" said the doctor. "Were you the coach-man who carried *him* off?"

"No, but there came a loud knock at Tom Walker's door one day, when the money-lender was grinding out of a poor man his last coin.   Tom Walker, as you know, went to the door, and what became of him?"

" The powers only know," said Dr. Oliver.

" There stood at the door a black man, with a black coach and black horses, and Tom Walker and the black man and the coach and the horses all vanished into the air, as quick as you could wink your eye, and his chests of gold were all found empty!"   The stage-driver glanced at the doctor.

" I wish that some power would take off Sam Adams in that way," said the doctor.   " If ever there was a ship of glass on a rocky sea, it is that man Sam Adams.   He has spent all of his fortune for liberty, as he calls it, and having nothing else to pass, he goes about passing resolutions."

A loon swept down and hooted near the doctor's head. He started up as if in terror.

" 'Twas a loon," said he, " that's all.   I didn't know but something was coming after *me*."

The stage-driver saw that the doctor was excited.   He resolved to add to his nervous fears.   So in a wild, deep tone he proceeded again to relate at length the old Boston wonder tale of the Devil and Tom Walker, and how the Evil One came and carried off the usurer at last.   The tale was a proverb against usury in old Boston for two generations, and has not quite yet ceased to be quoted.

Dr. Oliver was in a very fidgety mood for a time.   He

at last sat down, after many changes of place, among the
older boys, and said, as if absently :

" I never come down here that I do not get smoke and
charcoal dust on my hands, and the bother of it is that
common soap won't take off the grime. What do you
use, boys, for smutty hands?"

There were many answers. The doctor heard them
with seeming interest, then suddenly turned to Andrew
Fayreweather, and said:

" What do you use, Andrew?"

" Sea sand and salt water."

" Is that so? Well, I must try it, too. Did you really
ever use sea sand and salt water, or did some one tell you
that it was good?"

" I have tried it myself."

" You have, hey? Lately?"

" Yes."

" Within a day or two?"

" Yes."

" Is that so? Where did you get your sand?"

" Down by the wharf."

" Near by?"

" Yes, back of the blacksmith's shop."

" That so? Show! Did it work? Were your hands
very dirty?"

" Yes."

" Been handling coal or something, maybe?"
10

The doctor turned to Cameron, and said, in easy lan-guage:

"Gunpowder smoke is mighty hard to get off of one's hands or body. I once had it burned into me. I was once in a blacksmith's shop which blew up. You listen, boys, and I will tell you how it all was: Old John Early, who lived at Salem, went on the Shirley Expedition to Louisburg, and he used to drop into the Salem smithy at times, to tell of the wonderful doings at the time of the siege. One day he came around there with a paper of powder in his pocket. The blacksmith was pretty busy and active that day; the sparks flew, when all of a sudden up went the shop, and I was rolled over; and when I was taken up I was dreadfully burned. Look here!"

The doctor rolled up his coat-sleeve.

"The smoke was burned into me. See the marks of it there. Andrew, did you ever have any *powder* smoke on your hands?"

"Yes, I have."

"You have—lately?"

"Yes."

"How did it come there?"

A strange hesitancy came into Andrew's voice. "I—I—I——"

"Oh, never mind. Will sea sand and salt water take it out?"

"I—I—think likely."

"You say that you have tried them lately; how did it work?"

"Well——"

"It works well in cases of charcoal blackening and gunpowder?"

"Yes, sir. One gets gunpowder on one's hands handling guns," faltered Andrew.

"And *cannon?*" said Dr. Oliver. He bit the head of his cane. "They don't clean cannon here as they used to do when they were drilling for Louisburg," he added, in a distant tone.

The doctor usually employed impetuous but rather lofty language. He was *apparently* talking carelessly now.

"Andrew, come down to the wharf with me, and show me where you found that sand."

Andrew arose and led the way to the wharf, and pointed down to the open shore.

"Did you ever wash coal smut off there?" asked the doctor.

"Yes."

"So you said." The doctor leaned over the rail on the wharf, as if bent on some important discovery.

"And powder smut?"

Andrew hesitated.

"Why do you hesitate?"

"Yes, powder smut."

"Lately?"

Andrew hesitated again.

" What is passing before your mind, Andrew? You said that you had lately used the sand here for coal smut?"

" Yes."

" And powder smut?"

" Well, yes."

" Andrew Fayreweather, how did you get powder smut and coal smut on your hands in this particular place?"

" Why, you yourself said that you get your hands smutty here."

" But I don't.   I take care of my hands."

" But why did you say so?"

" I had my reasons."

" Dr. Oliver, this is not honorable."

" Not honorable!   Do you know to whom you are talking?   Andrew Fayreweather, I have been using a supposed case to read your conduct in the last two days. And I have read it.   You have used sea sand to wash away powder stains and charcoal stains.   What should a penman like you, in a counting-house, be doing with charcoal and gunpowder?   And down here by the black-smith's shop!   I hear that you have been away from your business of late.   I know how gunpowder soiled those white hands of yours, and afterward charcoal.   Andrew Fayreweather, look at me!   You know where the guns are hidden.   Tell me!"

"Never!"

"Never! Is that what you say to me? Never? Well, never mind; a pint of strawberries is as good as a barrel. Ay, ay, that's so! An eagle doesn't run around a farm-yard like a hen long—not very long. Ay, ay, my boy, I know you! The eagle is going to fly, and he will come swooping down again. I know you—ay, ay!—and you'll find out who I am before the stars set. That's so and *also!*"

Dr. Oliver, who had grown so nervous during Cameron's story, was exultant now. He went back to the smithy.

Cameron turned to Dr. Oliver as the latter came back, and said:

"Dogs know a sight."

"Yes," said the doctor, glancing aside. "That's so."

"And most things can be explained. I don't believe those two cannon went off in the way that the redcoats thought they did."

Blingo came to the door from his late work.

"Blingo," said Dr. Oliver, "where are the cannon?"

"The dog knows as well as I do," said Blingo.

"You may well say that," said Dr. Oliver. "You keep him around here most of the time. That's so!"

The doctor turned slowly away, saying:

"These stories are all very entertaining, boys. I'll come back again, and bring some of my friends with me. Ay, ay, that's so! There is a very evasive atmosphere about this place. Ay, ay! One can feel treachery in the dark. I will come back again. That's so!"

The doctor went up the hill as if in high spirits, repeating, " That's so! that's so!"

" Queue, Queue," called Blingo; " here, come in here. I may need you, good fellow; you may know much, but you can't talk."

The dog obeyed Blingo and entered the shop, and lay down by the warm forge.

CHAPTER XIV.

DR. OLIVER SEES A GHOST.

R. OLIVER did return, and that within an hour. With him he brought a British officer and two soldiers. Blingo's eyes grew larger and whiter than ever when he saw the four men.

The young men rose up in silence. It was a warm autumn night, and the wind now and then rustled amid the russet and yellow leaves of the great trees. But except the voice of the sea wind and the far cries of the night herons all was still.

"This way," said Dr. Oliver to the officer. "We will see the blacksmith alone first."

"You may wait there," said the British officer to the two soldiers. The latter were common soldiers, unarmed. They had possibly been summoned for the purpose of unloading the suspicious coal-bin.

Dr. Oliver took the officer to Blingo. He was met at the door by Queue, but the dog obeyed Blingo, and was quiet, though he remained inside the shop.

"This officer," said he to Blingo, "wants to have a

private conversation with you, and after that we may want to look around. I'll go out and talk with the boys."

Dr. Oliver came out of the shop, shutting the great doors behind him, but he did not talk with the boys. He walked to and fro breathing the cool air of the sea. The presence of the dog in the shop disconcerted him. He had a plan in mind that the dog might disturb.

There were low muttering sounds within the shop. These grew louder. Dr. Oliver stopped to listen. The young men and boys stood motionless. Queue growled.

" I will have you arrested, sir," the officer was heard to exclaim, suddenly, in a loud voice. " Do you mean to tell me, a British officer, that you will not allow my men to search this shop?"

Blingo's voice rose loud. " Do you see that?" Queue growled again.

There was a flash of fire above the door. Then there were shuffling sounds, and low words by Blingo, and growls by the dog, and silence.

Suddenly the door opened, and an amazing sight met the eyes of all. Two men seemed to rush out of the door, one as if carried upon the other's shoulders. The boots of the man who looked as though he were being carried protruded horizontally out of a great coat called in those days a "pea jacket," which seemed to be thrown over his body. His tall hat was tipped back, and his head seemed to be upturned, as in great distress.

It was a dusky night, and as the door opened the appearance of one man carrying another was very distinct as a rough, dark outline.

" Here he is!" uttered a gurgling voice. Whose?

Dr. Oliver, with lifted cane, stood as one petrified. The soldiers stood with open mouths, and the men and boys were wonderstruck.

" It is Blingo carrying off the officer," said Philip Fayreweather.

" It is the officer carrying off Blingo," said Andrew.

" But where is the uniform?" asked another.

The strange apparition as of two men, one carried away on the shoulders of the other, mounted the hill, when suddenly the two figures were transformed or sunk into one man, who ran over the hill and disappeared. The beholders stood for some moments in silence. Was the sentinel's story of the disappearance of the guns true? Were there witches still?

" That was Blingo himself," said Allie. " Where is the dog? Queue!"

" Boy," said Dr. Oliver, swinging his cane in a circle around his legs, " go, call the dog!"

" What did that mean?" asked one of the soldiers.

" Heaven only knows. I would say that tne days of witchcraft are not over yet," said the other. " One could believe anything after that!"

One of the soldiers looked into the shop. He saw there

only the dog, which seemed watching a great roll of leather.

"Blingo has escaped," cried the soldier. "Run, follow him."

"Yes, run, follow him," said Dr. Oliver. The two soldiers ran up over the hill, where the mysterious figure had gone. The boys ran after them. Dr. Oliver trudged on behind.

"Queue, Queue!" called Allie.

"Don't you call that dog," said Dr. Oliver. Then the doctor ran faster than ever. Then he suddenly stopped.

"What, ho! soldiers! "

The soldiers stopped.

"Where's Brant, the officer?"

Surely, where could he be?

"What are you doing?" cried Dr. Oliver. "Where is Brant?"

"Blingo carried him away," said the boys.

"He carried away Blingo," said the soldiers.

"But there was only one man when *they* reached the top of the hill," said Dr. Oliver.

"Look over the fence. Blingo has murdered him."

Allie called the dog, "Queue, Queue!"

The dog came bounding out of the shop. As soon as Dr. Oliver saw the dog his wits seemed to forsake him, and rushing up the hill, he cried, "Come on!"

At the top of the hill nothing was to be seen—neither Blingo nor Officer Brant.

"I've always heard that that blacksmith's shop was haunted," said Dr. Oliver, all out of breath. "I do believe that the witchcraft times are here again. That's what became of the two guns on the Common. The witches used to take Mercy Short up to the top of the room and hold her there. Blingo is a *wizard!*"

"We must go to the camp," said the soldiers. "It may be that Officer Brant is there." The men and boys followed the soldiers.

What strange thing had taken place? Two men had seemed to rush out of the shop and to become one man up on the hill, and then there was no man at all. All the witch stories of seventy-five years gone came back to the memory of every man and boy.

Dr. Oliver whirled around. His wits were coming back again.

"Allie, here! Allie Fayreweather! That dog ain't afraid of witches or anything. You and the dog come back with me. And you now keep the dog off of me. He won't trouble me as long as you are with him."

"What shall I go back for, Dr. Oliver?"

"I want you to go back with me. Nobody has seen Major Brant leave the shop. He may be there yet. Blingo may have killed him."

The two went back, the dog uneasily following them.

They came to the shop.   A great sheet of hide lay on
the floor, and it seemed to be moving.   The dog smelled
of it, and growled.

"That is the hide that Blingo straps up cattle with
when he shoes them," said Dr. Oliver.   "Look there, it
moves!   Was there ever such a night as this!   Let us go
in and look around."

The doctor went in and blew the fire with the bellows.
He then rested his hand, and cried:

"Major Brant!"

"Here, here, here!   Help, help, help—here!"

The voice came from the roll of leather.

Dr. Oliver ran toward the bundle.   Queue leaped before him, and growled.

"Allie, for humanity's sake unroll that leather heap."

Allie did so, and uncovered Major Brant.

"How came you there?" said Dr. Oliver.

"Where's the blacksmith?" asked the major.

"The witches have carried him away.   He's a wizard.
How came you here?"

"Dr. Oliver, I asked the blacksmith if the guns were
here, and he said they were not.   Then I asked him if
they had been here, and he would not say.   I then said,
'Blingo, I have come to arrest you.   I will call my men.'
He waved a fiery shovel over my head.   In a moment I
found myself thrown down, and rolled over in this hide,
and I heard Blingo say, 'If you move, the dog will make

an end of you.' Then I heard him put on some things and rush out. I could not call, for the dog stood growling over me. I would not pass again another such an hour of terror for all the world."

" Whom did Blingo carry away ? "

" No one; whom could he carry away ? "

" No one but himself. I see it all now, and how it was done. He put a pair of old boots on his hands," said Dr. Oliver, his brain clearing; "and he threw a cloak over his own shoulders sidewise, and tipped back his head, and made us all think that he was carrying you away on his shoulders." The doctor danced in indignation. "He is a wizard," said he. " He may be dead somewhere about here, and that may have been his apparition."

" Let us get out of this awful place," said Officer Brant. " Blacksmiths with fiery shovels, and dogs and spirits and wizards! You got me here, get me away—get me away!"

" That was Blingo's ghost that we saw," said Dr. Oliver, " or the Evil One has taken him off bodily. Only let me get home, and I'll stay there. Was there ever such a night as this! Talk of Mercy Short and—— "

" No, don't talk of Mercy Short," said Major Brant, " let's go."

Go they did. The dog ceased to be a terror to the doctor in view of these awful problems of his later imagination.

Blingo was heard of in Concord some days afterward, but he was never seen in Boston again until after the siege.

The doctor's solution of the stratagem was correct. Blingo, by putting an old pair of boots on his outstretched hands, and by throwing his great coat sidewise over his shoulders, and tipping back his head, had presented the appearance of *two* men, and in the dark had mystified all, by thus suggesting that the major was bringing out Blingo arrested, or that Blingo had shouldered the major, after a struggle between them.

The blacksmith's shop was searched the next day, and the bins showed where the cannon *had* been, but they were not there then.   A few of the young men knew where they were.   They soon were moved out of Boston in the wagons of compost, and went down the Concord roads.

CHAPTER XV.

AM ADAMS'S garden, which was despoiled during the occupation of the place by the British, was in the fulness of beauty now. The harbor glimmered through its trees, and its bowers were perpetually cooled by the vital sea-winds in summer.

The patriots used to gather there. Sam Adams loved its quiet. One June evening, in the longest days of the year, when the sky by day was one long melting splendor and the evening a hushed coolness of shadow and stars, he had stopped there to rest. He was a lover of music, and one of his musical friends came to see him, and to play the bass-viol and the violin. The neighbors were always welcome to the place, and one by one, hearing the music, came into the long enclosure and seated themselves near Mr. Adams. The more simple townspeople had come now to look upon Mr. Adams as a "prophet," one who somehow had been designated by fate to fulfil some inborn mission that the Divine Power only could understand.

Allie was the first to meet Mr. Adams on this beautiful June night.

"Mr. Adams," said the boy, playfully, "I have three wishes—only three."

"What are they, my boy?"

"May I have them?"

"I will see, my boy; first tell me what they are."

"The first is that the people's cannon may one day celebrate the departure of the British from Boston."

"You may have that, my boy. I think *that* day will come. Next, my boy?"

"That the cannon may celebrate the union of all the colonies as a free nation."

"A free and *independent* nation, my boy. It is an independent nation that I see in the future. Well, you may have that wish, my boy. That is a good one. What is the next?"

"That one day all the town may turn out to do you honor, and that I may lead the procession, and *drum*."

"No, no, my boy, that wish will not do. Sam Adams's ears were not formed for drum-sticks. No, no! But I like you for what you have said. This should be your third wish—that the colonies may proclaim to the world their independence, and that then you may lead a grand procession with your drum. You may have that wish. I think that that day will come; or it may be that I will be sent to London for trial; would you remember me then?"

The boy clasped the patriot's hand. The latter arose silently and led his little companion up and down the walk.

At this point the musician began to play again, and soon after, John Hancock, in velvet ruffles and gold lace, entered the yard, and sat down by Mr. Adams to enjoy the music.

Mr. Adams listened to-night as one to something that is far away. The dream of his life was haunting him. He was living, in fancy, in future and ultimate America. The joy of the seer was his. But he was organizing the new nation alone.

Mr. Holbrooke entered the growing company.

Mr. Adams greeted the master kindly, and told him the story of Allie's wishes and of his own wish.

"Master," said he, "you and your school have saved the four cannon for some cause; may they be fired if ever the colonies shall proclaim their independence. It seems to me that somehow there is destiny in those guns. When you put your foot on the wood-box you may not now know what you did. There is many a little event that leads to a great one."

He turned to John Hancock, who sat there, almost vainglorious, looking like an English peer at a royal reception.

Hancock lived in an elegant mansion on Beacon Hill, overlooking the Common and the harbor. The house was reproduced at the World's Fair in Chicago, and was known there as the Massachusetts Building. The original house stood near where the Massachusetts State House now stands, a little to the south, and rose from noble gardens and terraces. It commanded a view of the Charles and the Mystic Rivers, of the town and the sea. It had five stables, and John Hancock used to ride between this town house and his country house in Brookline in a coach drawn by six bay horses. It is said to his credit that he once met a washerwoman whom he knew, while riding in his princely style, and that he took her and possibly her clothes-basket to the place toward which she was travelling. It was also said in old Boston that he once met Sam Adams when the latter had been sued for debt, and that he gave him his sympathy and discharged his accounts. We hope these old tales were true.

Hancock was a rich man, fond of pomp and good living. Yet he had glorious ideals. In the siege of Boston, when it was thought that it would advance the cause to destroy the town, he sent a message to Washington: " Burn Boston if need be, and leave John Hancock a beggar!" Nothing could be more noble, unless it was the bold way in which he put his name to the Declaration of Independence. He was a very benevolent man, and was always great in spirit as long as he was under Adams's influence. He sleeps in the same graveyard as Adams, near the Park Street Church.

In the same house lived his noble wife, the famous
Dorothy Quincy Hancock, who, when the French fleet
suddenly came to Boston, caused all the townspeople's
pantries to be emptied, and all the cows on the Common
to be milked to entertain the polite French officers. The
old people of Boston used to relate that the French admi-
ral invited Madame Hancock and the ladies of Boston to
dine on the flag-ship; that Madame went with " five hundred of her friends"; that Madame was told to pull a certain cord when it should be time for the toasts to be said;
that Madame pulled the cord, and that the flag-ship went
bang! and that bang, bang, bang! went all the other ships,
and that Madame and her five hundred friends in silks and
feathers were greatly astonished and terrified, and that the
French officers bowed and bowed! What fine old times
those were!

But John Hancock was serious to-night. The courtier,
like the merchant, looked grave. He felt that he was in
the presence of a man of destiny.

" Mr. Hancock," said Mr. Adams, " great events are at
hand. I must meet the crisis, and you must support me.
We are not living for the present—we are living for the
future. Mr. Hancock, listen."

The man in ruffles bent forward his head. He was not
a great leader like Adams, but he had as noble impulses
and a lively imagination. Mr. Adams was now inspired
with visions of an American republic, and he grandly un-

folded them ; as he did at times to a few confidential friends.

" The very important dispute,"* said he, " between Britain and America has for a long time employed the pens of statesmen in both countries, but no plan of union is yet agreed on between them ; the dispute still continues, and everything floats in uncertainty. As I have long contemplated the subject with fixed attention, I beg leave to offer a proposal to my countrymen, viz., that a Congress of American States be assembled as soon as possible ; draw up a bill of rights, and publish it to the world ; choose an ambassador to reside at the British court to act for the united colonies ; appoint where the Congress shall annually meet, and how it may be summoned upon any extraordinary occasion, and what further steps are to be taken.

" The expense of an Annual Congress would be very trifling, and the advantages would undoubtedly be great ; in this way the wisdom of the continent might, upon all important occasions, be collected, and operate for the interest of the whole people. Nor may any one imagine this plan, if carried into execution, will injure Great Britain ; for it will be the most likely way to bring the two countries to a right understanding, and to settle matters in dispute advantageously for both. So sensible are the

* Mr. Adams's own words, but to another person.

people of America that they are in possession of a fine
country and other superior advantages—their rapid in-
crease and growing importance—it cannot be thought they
will ever give up their claim to *equal liberty* with any other
people on earth ; but rather, as they find their power perpetually increasing, look for greater perfection in just liberty and government than other nations or even Britain
ever enjoyed.   As the colonies are blessed with the richest treasures of nature, art will never be idle for want of
stores to work upon; and they, being instructed by the
experience, the wisdom, and even errors of all ages and
countries, will undoubtedly rise superior to them all in
the scale of human dignity, and give to the world new
and bright examples of everything which can add lustre
to humanity.   No people that ever trod the stage of the
world have had so glorious a prospect as now rises before
the Americans.   There is nothing good or great but their
wisdom may acquire, and to what heights they will arrive
in the progress of time no one can conceive.   That Great
Britain should continue to *insult* and *alienate* the growing
millions who inhabit this country, on whom she greatly
depends, and on whose allegiance in future time her existence as a nation may be suspended, is perhaps as glaring
an instance of human folly as ever disgraced politicians or
put common sense to the blush."

    " We must have relief," said Mr. Hancock, who saw the
vision of a republic in Mr. Adams's views at this time.

" It is then evident, if we have relief,* it must come from some other quarter.   It must result from the union and determined resolution of the colonies; they must force their unjust aggressors to comply with the dictates of reason.   It will perhaps be readily granted that there is no foundation to hope for redress of our grievances from Parliament.   But the question will be asked, How shall the colonies force their oppressors to proper terms?   This question has been often answered already by our politicians : ' Form an independent state,' '*an American commonwealth.*'   This plan has been proposed, and I can't find that any other is likely to answer the great purpose of preserving our liberties.   I hope, therefore, it will be well digested and forwarded, to be in due time put into execution, unless our political fathers can secure American liberties in some other way.   As the population, wealth, and power of this continent are swiftly increasing, we certainly have no cause to doubt of our success in maintaining liberty by forming a commonwealth, or whatever measure wisdom may point out for the preservation of the rights of America."

· Such were the visions of Sam Adams, whom his townsmen might well esteem as a prophet; and these visions history has fulfilled, and is fulfilling, and will ever fulfil.

We are now on the serious grounds of this great man's life.   The reader of fiction should be a student here.

* Mr. Adams's own words, but to another person.

Wells's "Life of Samuel Adams" presents a noble picture
of the statesman at this time, and we copy it:

"Samuel Adams followed an undeviating line in the
pursuit of American independence. Through storm and
sunshine, evil and good repute, he had kept this result
steadily in view, and seems to have yielded all else in life
to that one controlling idea. The writings of a lifetime
are devoted to the one aim of human liberty. All his
letters, essays, pamphlets, and state papers, everything that
emanated from his pen, centred upon that individual
object of his existence. Even the occasional writings on
religious topics bear as well upon civil freedom ; and all
the reports of his conversations and speeches are upon
political subjects. This treading one pathway for nearly
half a century would lead us to suspect a distaste for the
lighter fields of literature, did not the well-worn books
which remained in his library, and his evident acquaintance
with English authors, show that he could appreciate graces
of style as well as grandeur of sentiment. He keenly enjoyed life, in which his wants were few and easily supplied,
and his heart was full of sympathy for his fellow-men.
Nor can this adherence to one object be construed into
narrowness. In all else but his opposition to tyranny no
man was more liberal. He professed himself no bigot,
and respected the sentiment of adoration, under whatever
form or by whatever sect it might be felt. The concen-
tration of his faculties upon one idea was the mainspring

of his extraordinary power. All history illustrates that in art, discovery, literature, and invention, in every branch of science and the common pursuits of business, the diffusion of human capacity over a varied field of effort oftenest ends in defeat, when their direction upon a single great purpose leads to its accomplishment. We have already referred to the contemporary accounts of his style when addressing public assemblages. His personal ascendency among his fellow-members as a committeeman, and in touching the secret springs which produced results to the eyes of the world, was a strength of quite another kind.   In this respect, if we are to credit many contemporary witnesses, he had no equal in America. He has left nothing by which to show the working of this system; though one of his letters just after the signing of the Declaration modestly hints at 'the time and patience it had taken to remove old prejudices, to instruct the unenlightened, and to fortify the timid.' What has flashed from beneath the veil of secrecy leads to but one conclusion as to his ever active power."

Here is history for a young man to consider.

CHAPTER XVI.

"NO POWER ON EARTH."

HE town of Boston was now pulsing with excitement. The arrest of Sam Adams was daily expected. But the last of the Puritans walked the streets of Boston, followed by Queue, as calmly as on the Sabbaths of the early royal governors.

He was poor, and he seemed about to lose his noble estate on Purchase Street, with its beautiful gardens overlooking the sea. Attempts had been made to bribe him to support the vice-regal power. "Why has not Mr. Adams been taken off from his opposition, by appointment to an office?" asked a British minister of Governor Hutchinson. "Sir," said the ex-governor, "such is the obstinacy and inflexible disposition of the man that he never could be conciliated by any gift whatever."

He was sitting in his garden one day, looking off on the sea. There approached the house an elegant-looking officer, commanding one of the British regiments in Boston. Adams rose to meet him. Had this man come to arrest him, or to warn him of the danger of an arrest?

" Is this Mr. Adams ? " asked the officer.

" Samuel Adams, sir."

" Will you accord me the honor of an interview ?   I have a confidential communication for you from Governor Gage."

The two entered the house.

The officer noted that the buildings were out of repair. Money was surely needed here.

" This would be a most beautiful place that you have here, with some little improvements—a most beautiful place!   One could wish that you were more in harmony with the Castle and the Province House ; and I assume that that is the wish of the governor, that the leader of the people and the government should be friends, for so it ought to be in the interest of the peace and prosperity of the country.   I have been sent by the governor to express this wish to you."

" He is very considerate," said Mr. Adams, bowing.

" The governor not only sends me to express this wish to you in the interests of law and order and good administration of the necessary government, but he has commissioned me to ask you if there be any part in the government itself that you would accept in the interest of the harmony that should exist between the officers of the crown and the representatives of the people.   Office is honorable, and the remuneration for royal revenue is large."

" Sir," we may imagine Mr. Adams to have replied,

"I desire neither office nor money. Fame is air and money is dust, and luxury weakness of soul. I care for nothing but the cause of the American people. That fills me and thrills me; it is my food and my drink. Let me wear poor clothes, let my home go to decay, let them put a price on my head, and my grave be a bed of moss—what do I care, if I only live my life? You appear before me in gold lace, and I stand here in homespun. You hold your councils in gilded rooms, and I on the streets and in secret places. My duty lies with the future, and my council-chamber is the room where I meet my God."

Such, in substance, if not in real words, seems to have been Adams's spirit at this interview, that members of his family were ever pleased to recall.

"Governor Gage," said the officer, "offers you a place and a reward, that the colony may rest from dissension and be ruled in peace. What answer shall I return to him?"

We may here leave fiction and give what are probably Mr. Adams's own words:

"No personal consideration, sir, shall ever induce me to abandon the righteous cause of my country that I have espoused. Go, sir, and tell Governor Gage that it is the advice of Sam Adams to him that he no longer insult the feelings of an exasperated people."

The officer turned away. He had faced an incorruptible man. What was the Province House to this decaying estate? What was gold lace to this man's homespun clothing?

The last of the Puritans walked in his lovely gardens, and looked again out on to the blue, restless sea.

The wind blew, and the shingles flew from his barn, and he had no cloak of broadcloth and fur to wrap about him. But he owned himself, and he walked the highway that his soul made free.

A strange thing happened. The story sounds like a chapter of oriental fiction, but it is substantially true.

Some of his townsmen saw that his place was in need of repairs, and they came to him, and said:

" Mr. Adams, let us put a new covering on your house."

And the house was covered; how, the man of the town-meeting hardly knew.

Carpenters came and said: " Mr. Adams, we have been sent to rebuild your barn." The barn began to rise, and so many builders came that it was completed in a few days.

After he had been elected to the Continental Congress his townsmen began to see that his dress was rather plain. We let a writer of reminiscences tell the story of what followed. It reads like the Book of Job:

" There came to him certain persons and asked his permission to build him a new barn, the old one being decayed, which was executed in a few days.

" A second sent to ask leave to repair his house, which was thoroughly effected soon.

" A third sent to beg the favor of him to call at a tailor shop, and be measured for a suit of clothes, and choose his cloth, which were finished and sent home for his acceptance.

" A fourth presented him with a new wig, a fifth with a new hat, a sixth with six pairs of the best silk hose, a seventh with six pairs of fine thread ditto, an eighth with six pairs of shoes, and a ninth modestly inquired of him whether his finances were not rather low than otherwise.

" He replied that it was true that was the case, but he was very indifferent about these matters, so that his *poor* abilities were of any service to the public; upon which the gentleman obliged him to accept a purse containing guineas to support his present wants."

Glorious old Sam Adams! Where has thy spirit fled in these days of speculation and vainglory? Glorious old townspeople of Boston, who could so care for a man given to a cause! There is need that the Sons of the Revolution and the Daughters of the Revolution, and all young Americans as well who are not descendants of Revolutionary patriots, should study such characters as these.

" No personal consideration shall ever induce me—— "
Echo it, ye winds of time!

CHAPTER XVII.

HE Sons of Liberty were now secretly storing arms at Concord. There was an air of mystery in all the patriot clubs, and everywhere there was a thrill of suppressed excitement.

It was believed that the four guns had been sent to Salem or Concord; and wherever they were, Governor Gage had determined to find them, and to bring them back.

The boys' club which had pledged its honor to protect the guns had proved the beginning of other clubs, with a like purpose and more powerful, among which were the Incorruptible Thirty, whose leader was an enthusiastic patriot, with a name which became famous—Paul Revere.

Governor Gage sent couriers hither and thither to communicate with the Tories, as the royalists were called, in the country towns.

In the midst of the suspicion, excitement, and enforced preparation for war, the patriot schoolmaster was sitting at his desk late in the day. The days were lengthening;

the gates of the year were opening wider and wider to the sun; the birds had come to the Common again, and the old elm wore a hue of grayish green, which told that the season of bud and blossoms was near.

A horseman in homespun garb, on horseback, rode up to the schoolhouse and, bending over the side of the horse, peered through the front windows and beckoned to him.

The patriot schoolmaster hastened to the door.

"*Salem*," said the man.

"I understand," said the master.

"You are the man who put his foot on the wood-box where the guns were concealed?"

"I did that, and I sometimes think that that act is likely to lead to strange events. Where are the guns now?"

"I have been sent by Blingo to tell you that they are safe, and that we are sure that they will speak for liberty some day, and then you will be proud that you had put your foot on the wood-box. Blingo has sent me to say to you secretly that the guns and military stores are safe, and that if the British attempt to take them there will be *deep ploughing* in a certain field on that day. Do you understand?"

"I do understand."

"You will tell the boys and the Incorruptible Thirty."

The horseman turned away.

The patriot schoolmaster sat down at his desk again. There was war in the air, and in it his old pupils must

share, and some of them would have to stand by the guns
that they had hidden. He sat there until the sunset
flamed over the harbor, and the last rays shone on the
British flag over the Castle.

The wood-box was there; to his mind it grew and became a fortress, and his poor lame foot an army. There
have been fortresses and armies which never won for the
world such results as those humble instruments which now
filled the master's dreams.

The door softly opened. A black face appeared, full
of anxiety.

"Hist, hist! Massa Holbrooke yo' here, an' all alone?
Yo' may well be alone. Dese are still times. It is
great news I hab fo' yo'. We have heard from Massa
Adams. He's at Lexington, sho', an' he ain't comin'
back, Massa Holbrooke. Wot yo' an' yo' boys been
doin'? He ain't comin' back no more, an' Ole Surry's
heart it am done broke. An' John Hancock am wid him,
an' he is not come back. Lexington was his old home,
don't yo' know?"

"Yes, Surry; and what more have you heard?"

"Dat am all, an' dat be enough. Mis' Adams, she
walk de house an' look far away, an' say nuthin'. Dese
am troubled times, an' yo' has had part in dem, meddlin'
wid dose guns. Ole Surry wonders wot will happen next.
Dese yere am troubled times."

Old Surry went away with a "troubled" face.

It was the 18th of April, 1775. The city was quiet, but there was everywhere a sense that decisive events were at hand. The Incorruptible Thirty, under Paul Revere, had pledged themselves to watch the British soldiers, and to prevent a surprise at Concord, where the Sons of Liberty had been storing their guns and arms, and preparing for organization.

In the long twilight, Philip Fayreweather, one of the Incorruptible Thirty, came hurrying to the schoolhouse. The patriot schoolmaster was still there, writing copies in the many writing-books.

Philip opened the door, and without salutation said:

"The troops are going to move. They are collecting boats at the foot of the Common."

The schoolmaster arose.

"That wood-box haunts me," said he. "It looks to me as big as the Castle. I have fits of imagination as well as fits of the gout sometimes."

They went out on the hill on the Common which overlooked the then Charles River marshes.

Boats were indeed being gathered there—a little fleet of boats.

"They are for transports," said the master.

About ten o'clock a force of six hundred bayonets, grenadiers, and light infantry marched across the Common to the beach—a silent march, led by the British officers Colonel Francis Smith and Major John Pitcairn.

12

They glided away in the silence of that April night, and landed at Lechmere Point, now East Cambridge, and waded through the marshes, and then waited for some hours for their provisions to be transported to them.

This delay was fatal to their purpose.

Where were they going? To arrest Mr. Adams and Hancock at Lexington, and to seize the cannon and military stores at Concord.

Where was now Paul Revere, and where the old School Seven, and the Incorruptible Thirty?

Flash! What is that which gleams from the high belfry of the Old North Church? It is a signal-light! And who sees it? It is Paul Revere himself. He is mounted on horseback on the other side of the river, with an open way to Lexington and Concord.

Revere spurs his horse and starts over the country roads for Lexington to warn Adams and Hancock that the "regulars" are coming. But the regulars are riding, too. The special horsemen, who are expecting to surprise Adams and Hancock, are flying over the same road.

Revere has not gone far when he becomes aware that in speed alone is success.

He dashes forward. The moon rises, and the roads are light. At Medford he cries out to the minute-men, as the patriots who have pledged themselves to meet any emergency were called, and sets the church bells to ring-ing—clang, clang! in the deep hour of night. He shouts at every house as he passes, "Alarm, alarm! The regulars are coming!" Whip and spur, and that wild cry!

He sees the village of Lexington silent before him. He knows the house where Adams and Hancock are sleeping. He dashes up to the door.

The sentinel is dozing there.

"Alarm! Alarm!"

The sentinel jumps.

"Don't make such a noise, you will disturb the household!"

"Noise! You will have noise enough before long. The regulars are coming!"

A man puts his head out of the window.

"Revere, come in!"

It is Hancock.

Adams and Hancock prepare to flee, and Revere dashes on to Concord, screaming and setting the church bells of Lexington ringing.

That morning the regulars came marching down to Lexington, and they found the town awake and the minute-men awaiting them.

"Disperse, you rebels!" cried the maddened Pitcairn, with an oath.

They did not obey. The sun was rising—an April sun on the budding woods, orchards, and fresh fields—the sun of liberty.

There was a rattle of musketry. Blood was flowing;

men were falling on Lexington Green; the war was begun.

Adams heard the muskets on the near hills. The sun was now risen, and filling the valleys with light. Adams was not a poet, but he spoke one line on hearing the British volley as he listened on the hills, which is immortal:

" What a glorious morning is this!"

But in his dream of independent America Sam Adams on this glorious morning stood almost alone. The other patriots were thinking of their rights under the crown; *his* almost solitary vision was of an independent republic. And the American Republic of the future was embodied in Sam Adams, as he stood, prophet-like, on the hills, and uttered his only poem:

" What a glorious morning is this!"

When Governor Gage found that the expedition was discovered and being opposed, he sent Earl Percy, who came afterward to live in the Hancock House, to reinforce Smith and Pitcairn. The force under Percy started out of the town, by the way of Boston Neck, in gay regimentals and in high spirits, the drummer and fifer playing " Yankee Doodle." The tune, besides " Nancy Dawson " and " Lucy Locket," was also called " Chevy Chase," as an old Scottish ballad of that name had been adapted to it. Now Lord Percy belonged to the House of Northumberland, and the ballad of Chevy Chase celebrated the fall of the great leader of that house in the Scottish wars.

Where was Allie on this day of feverish excitement? He was a well-grown lad now, but he had not abandoned his drum. He wandered from place to place in search of news in the morning. He believed that the guns were at Concord, but he was not one of the Incorruptible Thirty; he was too young to be admitted to their secret councils. Would the guns be captured, or would they one day cause the British force to retreat before them?

On the morning of that day, the 19th of April, he passed along Boston Neck, on which the Conservatory of Music now stands, to Roxbury. The Neck had been fortified by Governor Gage, but he was not questioned by the guard at the gates. He sat down at last on a fence in Roxbury, in the sun, and looked down on the town and the harbor, and wondered if the regulars would return to the town by this way.

Suddenly he heard a sound of a drum and a fife. He started. The tune that the musicians were playing was none other than " Yankee Doodle." A troop came marching through the gates, with Earl Percy at their head. Allie knew that they must be going to Concord. He also knew that the minute-men of all the towns through which they would pass would be mustered to oppose them; that stone walls would be fortresses, and woods would pour forth musket-balls.

Lord Percy shone in a splendid uniform, and the British soldiers under him marched pompously as on dress parade.

Allie began to laugh at the pomp of the spectacle as he sat on the fence in the sun, and he continued to laugh and he clapped his hands on his knees as the troops danced past to the merry tune.

Lord Percy noticed him. The amusement of the boy excited his curiosity. He turned his head, and riding near the fence, shouted to Allie:

"And what are *you* laughing at?"

Allie started up.

"To think, sir, how you will look when you come back to the tune of ' Chevy Chase.' "

Lord Percy was a superstitious man. The words "Chevy Chase" struck him to the heart. It made him apprehensive all that day.*

But Lord Percy did come back, and so rapidly that the drummer and the fifer did not stop to play "Chevy Chase," nor any other tune. The regulars found their way back from Concord one long battlefield. Men fell on every hand from the muskets of a masked foe. They hurried faster and faster, and at last ran, and when they at night saw the lights of Boston town, it was with depleted numbers; and though some stores of war had been destroyed, the brass cannon which had been hidden in the gun-house had not been taken. They waited to be heard on Bunker Hill!

But they had drawn fire. The American Revolution had begun.

* The anecdote is historical.

Alla and Lord Percy.

CHAPTER XVIII.

HE guns are at Cambridge. Volunteer, and you will find them there. Some of you have saved the guns; now they are waiting for all of you to handle them and to proclaim Liberty through them. Volunteer!"

So said the patriot schoolmaster to the Younger Sons of Liberty, who had gathered in the old schoolhouse after the contest of Lexington and Concord. The room echoed with the word " Volunteer!"

Among the people associated with the thrilling movements of the times whose names are historic was Moses Grant, who became a deacon of the Brattle Street Church. He was one of the Boston Tea Party, and one who helped to spirit away the guns on the Common. Another of these mysterious persons, whose names afterward appeared, was Dr. Elisha Story, of whom Drake in his " Tea Leaves " writes thus:

" Dr. Elisha Story led a party of young men to the Common, where there was a sentinel guarding two field-pieces. While Story overawed the sentinel by presenting a pistol to his head and enjoined silence upon him, the others came behind and dragged away the guns, one of which was afterward placed in Bunker Hill Monument."

We have given Dr. Story's stratagem the enlargement of fiction in a former chapter. The men and the boys of the patriotic clubs, who had saved the guns, were now re-solved to make them a power for right and for liberty, and most of those people were present and cheered the patriot schoolmaster's words.

"The guns are at Cambridge!" The master's words were thrilling. The men wished to see them. The war had begun with the guns.

"Master Holbrooke, you held the Castle when you put your foot on that wood-box," said Dr. Story. "Now let us hold the Castle by putting the guns on the hills around Boston. Who will volunteer?"

The word seemed to thrill the very air. The whole company rose, and shouted, "I—I—I—I!"

General Artemus Ward had been appointed the com-mander-in-chief of the military forces around Boston by the Massachusetts Provincial Congress, which Congress was largely the creation of Sam Adams. He was organ-izing a provincial army at Cambridge. The towns of New England were full of volunteer companies and minute-men. These were hastening to Cambridge. An army of more than twelve thousand men was gathering there. It was the purpose of General Ward to fortify the circle of hills around Boston; to cut off supplies to the British army by land, and to compel the British to evacuate the place.

Lord Howe had arrived in Boston just before this crisis, to reinforce Governor Gage. Lord Howe was an uncle of George III. He came to Boston in May, 1775, with a disciplined army and high-born officers, and took command of all the British forces.

General Ward had begun to make preparations to fortify the hills near Charlestown, overlooking the town of Boston, and with the arrival of Lord Howe thrilling events were near at hand. The British army in Boston and the patriot army gathering at Cambridge were nearly equal in numbers, but the one army was trained and the other awkward and undisciplined, yet afire with will and zeal.

The patriot schoolmaster, who had hidden the guns, Dr. Story, who had held in terror the sentinel, and the boys, who had resolved to protect the gun-house from robbery, formed an earnest company. It was a May evening, and the lights were low. Suddenly there strode into the room a giant form. His steps rang, and his arms swung to and fro. He turned and faced the company, and said:

"I have done my duty, now you do yours. I must be gone."

The giant strode to the door, and cried, "Cambridge!" It was Blingo, the blacksmith. He went out, and van-

ished like the guns which Dr. Story had caused to disappear.

Every one present was now eager to hurry to Cambridge. The word was a watchword. "Cambridge!
Cambridge!" rang through the dusky room.

"How many of you are ready to volunteer for Cambridge?" asked the master.

The whole school arose.

"All; but a part of you must remain here, to guard
your own homes, and to provide for the dependent. What
do I see before me? Ten of you who have volunteered
for this service are the sons of sailors' widows. The
Widow Fayreweather has three sons here. Only one of
the older boys ought to go."

"It is my mother's wish that I go," said Andrew
Fayreweather.

"Let me determine who shall offer themselves for this
service," said Master Holbrooke. "You see my school-
bag here, and the corn that we have stored under the
desk for our noon parties in stormy weather? There are
a few red ears among the corn. There are four families
here represented by brothers who have widowed mothers.
I am about to do a curious thing. I will put four red
kernels of corn and six white kernels of corn into this bag.
I will then blindfold the ten volunteers whose fathers are
dead, and let each of the brothers of each family while
blindfolded draw out of the bag a kernel of corn. If each

brother of the same family draws a white kernel, each shall put back the kernel into the bag, and all shall draw in this way until one brother of each family shall have drawn a red kernel of corn. Those who draw a red kernel shall offer themselves as cannoneers in the service of those guns."

A thrilling scene followed. All were eager to go.

" Andrew and Philip Fayreweather!"

The two young men stepped before the master, who bandaged their eyes.

" Andrew Fayreweather, draw."

The young man put his hand into the bag and drew out a kernel of corn.

His brother bent toward him blindfolded, and whispered in his ear:

" Do not show your kernel of corn until I have drawn mine. I have a secret reason for asking it. Remember."

Andrew, not comprehending his brother's meaning, held the kernel of corn lightly in his hand, and lifted the bandage with the other. " What have you drawn?" asked the master.

" I do not know. It is there in my hand. I propose to show it later."

He held up his hand in view of all.

" Philip Fayreweather, draw."

Philip put his hand into the bag and drew out a kernel of corn. He quickly lifted the bandage, and saw that it was white. It had not been observed that he had made this discovery, for his movements had been quick, cautious, and nervous. Philip thought of Annie. He had no sweetheart: if Andrew could be kept at home, he would be free to give his own life to the cause.

" Andrew," said he, clasping his brother's hand, in which was the concealed kernel, " have we both drawn white corn ? "

Andrew drew his hand away from his brother's strong grasp, and offered the hand in view of all. In it was a white kernel of corn.

" I am glad it is white, for mother's and Annie's sake," said Philip. " I hope that mine is red."

He stood apart from all, lifted his arm, and opened his hand. It was a red kernel of corn.

Philip and his brothers went to his home from the schoolhouse. Their mother met them at the door. The family sat down before the fire.

" Mother," said Philip, " I have done a thing that may cause your face to fall."

" No dishonor, I hope, Philip ? "

" I am going to Cambridge. I am going to fulfil my promise to stand by the guns."

" You do honor to your name, Philip; you have a brave heart. The blood of your dead father is in it. Go, God bless you, go !"

" Can you do without me, mother ? "

The widow arose.

"Do without you? Yes. These hands have become used to work. Do without you? I can do without you all!"

"Without me too, mother?" said Allie.

"Yes, my boy; you may go and drum."

"I drum for Sam Adams," said Allie, using a favorite expression.

"And for more than that," said his mother. "Mr. Adams is called to no ordinary work in the world, mark you that, my boys; I can see it. Samuel Adams was born for all mankind."

"I shall stay by you, mother," said Andrew.

"You need not; yet for Annie's sake I would be glad to have it so. But the cause of God stands before all other things. I would have my boys live for all that is best. Death is nothing, empty homes are nothing, so but the right prevail."

She stood there in silence, with her eyes lifted.

"O mother!" said Philip, with tears in his eyes.

She laid her arm on his shoulder, and looked into his eyes. The mother and son had embraced each other for the last time.

Washington came to Cambridge after the battle of Bunker Hill, and took the formal command of the American army there on the 3d of July. The old elm still stands near Cambridge Common where he first met the army. In the top of the tree was his lookout, from the platform of which he watched from time to time the movements of the army of Lord Howe in the town. It was the influence of John and Samuel Adams which intrusted to Washington this great command, for American liberty and for all mankind.

Lexington was a bugle blast. The patriots of all the colonies heard it. In a few weeks an army of untrained but resolute men gathered around Boston. The volunteers came flying from the farms to drive the British army " into the sea." Israel Putnam, in his leather waistcoat, came from Connecticut, John Stark from New Hampshire, and Nathanael Greene from Rhode Island. The new army began to prepare to fortify the hills around Boston.

It was this army that Philip saw gathering when he reported to the headquarters of General Ward.

The army was encamped in the fields near Harvard College, and on the banks of the Charles and Brighton meadows. It was May.

Philip sought the artillery. The four guns were there. How came they there? He would find Blingo.

This was an easy thing to do. Blingo was at his post of duty, which was that of a cannoneer.

" Blingo, the guns are here!"

" The guns are here, as you see."

" I have come to fulfil the promise I made in the writing-schoolhouse. I want to volunteer in some service in the battery. Can you help me?"

" I can, and will."

" But, Blingo, how did the guns get here?"

" The carters took them out of the town, under their loads; the rest was easy."

Philip was accepted as a volunteer for the battery service, or field-gun service, for field-guns the cannon really were. He was put to drill. In a few days he was joined by other members of the old school club. They were to be subject to any duties required of them.

The army about the 16th of June numbered some fifteen thousand or more men. Troops continued to pour in, but a great many of them were without arms, save those which nature had provided. Should they fortify the heights overlooking Boston? The patriots turned for an answer to the field-pieces. These said: "Yes! Go, and we will follow you!"

On June 15th the Committee of Safety, acting as a military directory, ordered the fortification of Breed's Hill and of Bunker Hill. The two hills were a part of the same elevation. On the evening of the 16th a body of Massachusetts troops and two cannon went forward to intrench. Nine o'clock found this division at Breed's Hill. The rest of the army remained at Cambridge. Philip and Blingo were ordered to go with the intrenching army.

At midnight the advance troops began to throw up intrenchments for siege guns, under the direction of Generals Putnam and Prescott.   It was a silent army of spade-
men, so silent that the officers could hear the British sentinels over the river say to each other, "All is well."

"One o'clock," the sentinels said, "All is well," in
deep-toned voices; "two o'clock, all is well," in sleepy
voices; "three o'clock, and all is well: all is well."

The morning came.   It was about the time of the longest
days of the year—June 17th.   The gray light whitened
the sea, and the sky began to lift its arches of red.

"All is well?"   No, false sentinels, all was not well for
the sleeping army in Boston.   A salvo of artillery awoke
the town, and the British officers looked across the Charles
and Mystic in amazement.   A redoubt threatened the
town.

Blingo and Philip, who had left the field-pieces at Cambridge, under orders to follow the night march and to prepare intrenchments to cover the main army, surveyed the
town and talked of the strange movement of events.

The enemy were now awake and preparing for defence.
A frigate and floating batteries moved into the basin of
the Charles River.   Other naval forces followed.

The battery was reinforced by two ship-guns; but the
intrenching tools had gone to a higher point, called Bunker
Hill.

"What can we do with the new guns?" asked General

Prescott. " There are no embrasures from which to fire them, and the tools are gone."

" Let the soldiers dig intrenchments with their hands," said the officer addressed.

Blingo and Philip thrust their hands into the earth. The soldiers followed them; the embrasures were made.

Philip rose up from his work.

" Look at my hands," said he. They were dripping with blood.

In the afternoon the British army crossed the river and landed under the cover of guns from the ships. It came in magnificent array, under the command of Lord Howe.

A portion of the American army moved from Cambridge on receiving the news that the British were landing. They were compelled to march under the fire of the British guns as they approached the two hills. They brought the field-pieces.

The battle began, the American lines closing the peninsula from river to river, defended by the redoubt and the field-pieces. It was nearly four o'clock in the afternoon. The purpose of Howe was to first capture the redoubt.

Howe sent a message to General Burgoyne, who commanded the cannon at Copp's Hill near the church from which the lanterns were hung for Paul Revere, to burn Charlestown. The cannon were turned on the town, and it soon burst into flames.

The British bugles sounded, and the gleaming army

13

pressed toward the provincials, under the bright sky of the late June afternoon.   It was a moment of horror to the farmer soldiers.   The line came on, the officers waving their swords toward the redoubt.

The Americans were silent.   They had scanty stores of ammunition.

"Do not fire until the British are within thirty yards," was the order which passed from company to company.

The gleaming line moved up to the crisis of the onset upon the redoubt.

" Fire!"

Whole companies of British soldiers seemed to reel and fall.

" Back!" said Howe.

The British fell back.   The smoke lifted.   The attack had failed.

A loud huzza arose from the American ranks.

The lull in the battle revealed an awful sight: the roofs and the church spires of Charlestown were falling amid columns of flame; ships were blazing at the wharf, and the cannon were thundering over the river.

A second assault soon followed the first, and the British were again driven back.

The final struggle was now near at hand.   The British were receiving reinforcements, but the ammunition of the Americans was nearly gone.

Philip Fayreweather stood in the redoubt.   It was near

night. He knew that the ammunition of the Americans was nearly spent, and that the next assault might fill the place with dead and gory men.

" I am ready to fall," said he to Blingo. " I may be the first to go down for the cause that I promised to defend in the gun-house. The cause, the cause! All that I care for is the cause!"

Prescott rode up. He looked like a man whose soul was aflame. " Keep your fire," he shouted, " and do not waste a grain of powder!"

The commander of the redoubt stood awaiting the third charge. The men stood by him in silence. The scarlet line was moving again. It swept up to the trenches The redoubt remained as still as the twilight sky. Then it again poured forth the fires of death. The enemy reeled, but the powder of the Americans was gone. The redcoats came leaping over the parapets and fired into the very faces of the patriots. Men fell in heaps. The patriots used their bayonets, hurled stones, and seized the guns of their assailants. But the four walls of the redoubt were at last surrounded.

" Save yourselves!" cried Prescott.

The redoubt was crowded with the dead and the dying. The patriots who could do so fled with their empty guns.

" Come on!" shouted Blingo to Philip.

" Stay, I am wounded," was the answer.

The young soldier sank down, the blood flowing from his neck.

" No, go!" he said. " I may as well die alone. I wish for but one thing."

" You shall have it, if it costs me my life," said Blingo.

Philip sank down amid the dying. The red twilight was fading slowly. The guns had ceased. Groans and cries of anguish arose on every hand.

" Blingo," said Philip, " save yourself."

" I will never leave you!" answered the heroic black-smith.

" Blingo, I can walk; lead me away to the guns which I swore to guard. They will not shoot one leading away a bleeding man."

The stars came out and shone through the smoky air.

Blingo arose, and led Philip down the hill toward the lights of Cambridge. He was not molested.

The cool winds came in from the sea. Night, merciful night, was shadowing the hills and the two rivers.

" Blingo, I can go no farther. Let me lie down."

Blingo laid him down on the dewy grass.

" Bring me water, Blingo."

But where was water to be found? Blingo started toward the nearest light.

" Stop, Blingo, it is of no use. You do pity my mother, don't you? She is a brave woman. Tell her that I died as a soldier should, and that I am glad that I did my duty. It is not a long life or a short life, Blingo, which counts, but to do one's duty."

The winds grew cooler, and he breathed heavily. A spasm seized him: he rallied.

"Tell Andrew that I love him, and that I have always loved him more than he can know. I wish I could be buried in the Granary Burying-ground under the trees, for, Blingo, I am dying. Could you carry me to one of the field-pieces and lay me down there?"

The giant blacksmith took the bleeding young soldier in his arms and bore him to the field-pieces, and there laid him down.

"I can die now," he said: "I have kept my word."

Near midnight his soul passed; when, Blingo did not know. All night Blingo sat by the still form, now and then putting his hand over his heart to see if indeed it were motionless.

The first light revealed the face of death. Blingo closed the eyes and went for assistance. They buried him there in the field. The hands of love would remove his body when peace should come.

CHAPTER XIX.

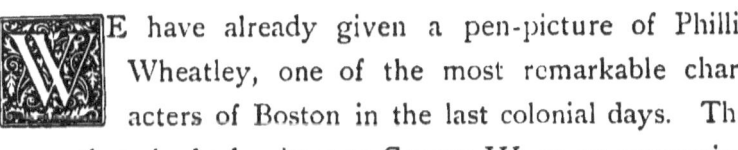E have already given a pen-picture of Phillis Wheatley, one of the most remarkable characters of Boston in the last colonial days. The poem that she had written to George III. as an expression of gratitude for the repeal of the Stamp Act had made her very famous, and on the arrival of Washington at Cambridge she had a new inspiration to write a poem to the commander-in-chief of the American army. The name of "Washington" rang through Boston in the winter of 1775–76.

One day Phillis appeared at the Adams mansion, her eyes all sparkle and her cheeks all aglow.

" Is dat yo', Phillis ? " said good Old Surry. " Who did yo' come to see ? "

" Mrs. Adams," said the sprightly colored girl, with an air of importance.

" Mis' Adams, it am her yo' hab come to see ? Yo' look mighty chipper, Phillis. Wot yo' been doin' ? "

"I have written a poem, and I have come to read it to Mrs. Adams, and perhaps to Mr. Adams."

"Been writtin' mo' poetry, Phillis? Who to?"

"It will surprise you, Surry. Whom to? Whom should it be to?"

"Massa Adams, Phillis; he's a prophet, he is now. If yo' could see him goin' around mumblin', mumblin', mumblin', yo' would know dat his head was in de stars. Massa Adams, to be sho', who else, Phillis?"

"No, the Muses didn't inspire me to write to Mr. Adams this time."

"'The Muses'? Who is dem? De goosies? I never heard tell of no muses. Why didn't they 'spire yo' to write to Massa Adams? Dey do say dat he belongs to de family of Adamses one reads about in de Bible; an' I do tink dat he jest is de most glorious man of dese yere latter days. He talks jest like chapters out of de Ole Testament. If not Massa Adams, who den?"

"To Washington—the great Washington himself."

Old Surry raised her hands. "Bress de Lor'! An' wot yo' goin' to do wid it, Phillis, after yo' read it to Mis' Adams?"

"What if I were to take it over to Cambridge and read it to Washington himself?"

Old Surry sank into a chair and lifted both hands, and said: "Now I am done beat! To Washington hissel'! He would put you in de guard-house, Phillis."

" I guess not; I have a letter from him."

A bust of Phillis Wheatley, the first American colored poet, was made in Paris by a well-known artist as a tribute to the earliest genius shown in America by one of the African race. The sculptress, Miss Edmonia Lewis, of Paris, is herself a colored woman, and the bust was made for a place at the World's Fair, through the influence of the colored women of Alleghany County, Pa.

The life of Phillis Wheatley, whom Washington received and commended at his headquarters in Cambridge, Mass., in the early days of the Revolution, just before the evacuation of the city of Boston by the British troops, reads like a romance of fiction, and represents so much worthy influence that we are glad that an interest in it was revived by the bust made for the White City.

As we have intimated in an earlier chapter, where Phillis Wheatley was born or what her real name was no one ever knew or can know. She was stolen from her home on the coast of Africa in the days of the slave-trade, and was brought to Boston in a slave-ship in the year 1761. Here she was offered for sale. She was purchased by the wife of Mr. John Wheatley.

This lady held several slaves, who were growing old. She wished to have a bright girl about her whom she might educate and train as a companion for her old age.

" Phillis," as she was called, was not handsome, but

she had a remarkable forehead, and an air of unusual intelligence. Her face was peculiar, but there was genius in it.

This wild African girl, who came to be received by some of the most notable people of England and America, had only a dirty piece of carpet for a covering when she was landed in Boston, and was advertised for sale like an animal.

She was then about seven years of age. Mrs. Wheatley gave her her own name, and took charge of her education. Phillis was quick as a scholar, and was found to possess the poetic sense and vision. She said that the only thing of her African life that she seemed to remember was a custom of her mother in pouring out water from some vessel before the rising sun.

She developed a thirst for knowledge, learned Latin, and came to love the Latin poets. She began to write verse, following the Virgilian methods of personification. With the growth of slavery in the country came a prejudice against her development of genius, and what it represented. Her work was much praised or greatly disparaged. A new interest has lately been awakened in the poetess, but her work must always be judged by the circumstances under which it was produced.

She went to London, and while she was there waiting to be presented to the court of George III. news reached her that her mistress was ill. She returned to America

to attend Mrs. Wheatley in her last days.   Mrs. Wheatley died in 1774.

Phillis married a colored man by the name of Peters,
and her life from that time became one of hard work, des-
titution, and suffering.   She died somewhat later than the
year 1784, but the exact year of her decease is not known.

The reader will doubtless like to see some specimens of
the verse of this remarkable woman.   We will give some
extracts from " To Mæcenas," the patron of Roman literature.   The " Terence " of whom she speaks was a Roman
writer of African birth.

> " Mæcenas, you, beneath the myrtle shade,
> Read o'er what poets sung and shepherds played.
> What felt those poets, but you feel the same?
> Their noble strains your equal genius shares,
> In softer language and diviner airs.
>
>   .   .   .   .   .
>
> " Great Maro's strain in heavenly numbers flows,
> The *Nine* inspire, and all the bosom glows.
> Oh could I equal thine and Virgil's page,
> Or claim the Muses with the Mantuan sage,
> Soon the same beauties should my verse adorn,
> And the same ardors in my mind should burn ;
> Then should my song in bolder notes arise,
> And all my numbers pleasingly surprise.
> But here I sit and mourn a grovelling mind,
> That fain would mount, and rise above the wind!
>
> " Nor you, my friend, these plaintive strains become,
> Nor you whose bosom is the Muses' home.

When they from towering Helicon retire
They fan in you the bright immortal fire;
But I, less happy, cannot raise the song—
The faltering music dies upon the tongue.

" The happier Terence all the choir inspired,
His soul replenished and his bosom fired.
But say, ye Muses, why this partial grace
To one alone of Afric's fabled race,
From age to age transmitting thus his name
With the first glory in the rolls of fame?

        .   .   .   .   .

" As long as Thames in streams majestic flows,
Or Naïads in their oozy beds repose,
While Phœbus reigns above the starry train,
While bright Aurora purples o'er the main,
So long, great sire, the Muse thy praise shall sing—
So long thy name shall make Parnassus ring.
Then grant, Mæcenas, thy paternal rays,
Hear me propitious, and defend *my lays!*"

As a poet she loved the vocative case, like the Greek
and Latin singers. On leaving New England she writes:

" Adieu, New England's smiling meads,
    Adieu, the flowery plain;
I leave thy opening charms, O Spring,
    And tempt the roaring main.

" In vain for me the flow'rets rise
    And boast their gaudy pride,
While here beneath the northern skies
    I mourn for *health* denied."

Phillis Wheatley, at a very interesting historic period, once wrote a very ingenious and finished *rebus*. We copy it, and will leave the reader to admire the skilful literary work, and to *guess* the word:

> " A *bird* delicious to the taste,
> On which an army once did feast,
>   Sent by a hand unseen;
> A *creature* of the horned race,
> Which Britain's royal standards grace;
>   A *gem* of vivid green;

> " A *town* of gaiety and sport,
> Where beaux and beauteous nymphs resort,
>   And gallantry doth reign;
> A *Darden hero* famed of old
> For youth and beauty, as we're told,
>   And by a monarch slain;

> " A *peer* of popular applause,
> Who doth our violated laws
>   And grievances proclaim.
> The *initials* show a vanquished town
> That adds fresh glory and renown
>   To old Britannia's fame."

Such is briefly the history of a person whom we have introduced in the former part of this story, and who is now planning to recite her work to Washington himself.

Phillis strode firmly into Mrs. Adams's room and bowed deferentially to that lady, while Old Surry stood listening at the door.

"I have here a very important letter, Mrs. Adams, very important to me; and it has made Mrs. Wheatley very proud."

"Whom is it from, Phillis?"

"From General Washington."

"Is it for Mr. Adams?"

"No, Mrs. Adams."

"Whom is it for?"

"It is for *me*."

"What does it say, Phillis?"

"General Washington has invited me to visit him at his headquarters."

"How came he to do that, Phillis?"

"I wrote a poem and sent it with a note to him, and asked him if he would receive me."

"Read his answer, Phillis."

Phillis read a most polite and elegant note addressed from the army headquarters at Cambridge.

Mrs. Adams was very much surprised. As for Old Surry, when she heard Phillis read the note, she said:

"Yo' Phillis, Phillis Wheatley, go slow now. I can hardly keep my turban on de top of my head for wonder. Wot yo' surprise me dat way fo'?"

The letter was as follows:

"CAMBRIDGE, Feb. 28, 1776.

"MISS PHILLIS: Your favor of the 26th of October did not reach my hands till the middle of December. Time enough, you will say, to have given an answer ere this. Granted. But a variety of important occurrences, continually interposing to distract the mind and withdraw the attention, I hope will apologize for the delay and plead my excuse for the seeming but not real neglect.

"I thank you most sincerely for your polite notice of me in the elegant lines you inclosed; and however undeserving I may be of such an encomium and panegyric, the style and manner exhibit a striking proof of your poetical talents, in honor of which, and as a tribute justly due you, I would have published the poem, had I not been apprehensive that while I only meant to give the world a new instance of your genius I might have incurred the imputation of vanity. This, and nothing else, determined me not to give it a place in the public prints.

"If you should ever come to Cambridge or near the headquarters, I shall be happy to see a person so favored by the Muses, and to whom Nature has been so liberal and beneficent in her dispensations.

"I am, with great respect,

"Your obedient and humble servant,

"George Washington."

"Read me dat letter again," said Old Surry, as Phillis left Mrs. Adams's room. "Tink of de great General Washington doin' dat, an' to yo', Phillis! Why, when yo' landed in Boston, all de clo' yo' had was an ole piece of carpet wrapped aroun' yo'; dat was all, Miss Phillis! dat the way yo' begin. Wot do it say about dat poetry?"

"'The elegant lines,'" repeated Phillis, proudly.

"Wot was it he say about yo' talons, Phillis?"

"'Your poetical talents,'" read Phillis. "He says that, while he would be unwilling to publish a poem written in praise of himself, the style and manner of my poem exhibit a striking proof of my poetical talents. Do you understand?"

"Course I understands; who do yo' take me fo'? De time may come when General Washington will enter Boston, de guns all boomin', an' de flags all flyin'. Wouldn't yo' feel great den, Phillis? An' maybe he would bow to me. I would bow to him; he couldn't help dat, now could he, Phillis?"

"It is not all education," said Mrs. Adams, entering upon the scene; "to have gifts is a great thing. Washington could not bow to many who have received a greater gift than you have, Phillis. Be humble and thankful. Poets are prophets, and it is such that glorify the world."

"Do yo' hear dat, Phillis?" said Old Surry. "It am de greatest ob. all things to hab de gifts ob de heabenly worl'."

The headquarters of Washington were at the Craigie House, Cambridge, which afterward became the home of Longfellow, the poet. It remains to-day as in colonial times.

Phillis went there somewhat timidly, it is likely, but Washington received her most graciously. No doubt the poem was written in the pompous Latin style, and greatly extolled his greatness and virtues. It would be a curiosity to see this poem, but it never was found among Washington's papers. But Washington's kind and beautiful reception of the unfortunate child is one of the things that

the old Boston story-tellers loved, when they livened their
fires and talked of Revolutionary days. It was alike noble
for Washington to appreciate this girl's gifts and to never
allow the personal flattery of the poem to meet the public
eye.

Poor Phillis, how she must have felt as she left the
Craigie House! We can imagine the scene as she stood
near the house under the spreading elms: the black girl
with her beaming face, and the general's stately bow as,
hat in hand, he thanked her for "the honor," and bade
her good-by under the purple sky of the returning spring.

"May you ride in triumph through Boston," said the
girl, weeping, as she went toward the bridge.

Phillis's reception by Washington was one to make Sam
Adams's heart glad, but Old Surry heard the tale with
renewed wonder.

The two colored women soon met, the one educated, the
other quaint, but both honored by the families in which
they lived.

"Phillis, yo' Phillis," said Old Surry, "yo' may live to
see General Washington ridin' into Boston some day, on
his prancin' horse. Massa Adams, he say so. How will
yo' feel then? How yo' feel, wid dose four cannon dat
were in de gun-house all boomin' from de four hills, an'
de people all shoutin', an' yo' de poet of it all! I can
see it now in my mind's eye, like Massa Adams—he sees
things. O Phillis, de drums will roll an' de hills will
tunder!"

CHAPTER XX.

ALLIE FAYREWEATHER was a manly, gentlemanly boy. He had been well taught by his mother as to the duty and respect that he owed to his superiors. He was never disrespectful to Dr. Oliver, but the latter seemed to form a most bitter prejudice against him on account of his partiality for Sam Adams. The doctor was a very arbitrary man, and unreasonable when his passion was excited. He was very self-willed, and long held to his resentments.

He had resolved to punish Allie with his cane when the boy had refused to tell him all that he knew in regard to the guns. He waited an opportunity when he should find him alone. He used to meet Allie at times when the boy was with others, and he would turn around to follow him with his eye, and shake his cane, and exclaim :

" I'll be even with you yet. Ay, ay!"

Allie knew that the doctor only waited a chance to meet him alone to punish him. He avoided him in every

14   195

way that he could; he had done nothing wrong, but he
lived in terror of the long cane which the doctor shook at
him whenever they saw each other.   "Ay, ay!" rang in
his ears.

One day the doctor met Allie on the Common where
the old graveyard now is.   The marshes bordered the
Common then.   Allie did not see him until the revengeful
cane was swinging above him in the air.   But he glided
away from the blow.   Queue was near him.   •

"Queue, Queue!" Allie called as he ran.   The dog
bounded after him.

The doctor was so angered by the boy's escape that he
threw his cane after him with the greatest force.

It did not hit Allie, who now ran faster than ever.   But
Queue turned around and seized the cane in his mouth,
and carried it away after Allie.

The doctor was now more furious than before.

"Stop!" he cried. • "Stop, you thief!"

Allie heard the word "thief," and turned around.

"Here, you bring back that cane, or I'll have you in
jail before the sun goes down.   Bring back that cane, or
I'll have the officers after you, Allie Fayreweather; you
take that cane from the dog and bring it here, and don't
you wait one minute.   These are high times, when a boy
steals a man's cane right before his eyes like that.   Bring
it back, I say, bring it back!"

Allie stood still, filled with terror.   What should he do?

To carry back the cane would be to invite a terrible punishment, which he did not deserve. Only the dog would prevent it. A quick thought struck him.

" Queue, Queue," said he, pointing, " carry it back— back—back!"

Queue turned toward the doctor with the cane in his mouth. The doctor was as afraid of the dog as Allie was of the doctor.

Queue stood before the doctor with the cane in his mouth, and looked up into his face. The doctor bent over very cautiously, but he hardly dared to take it from the dog's mouth.

" Drop it, drop it!" said the doctor.

The dog looked up at him but did not obey him.

" Here, you boy, you come here, and make the dog drop that cane, or I'll have you both arrested. There never was a time of such impudence as this in the whole creation—do you hear what I say?—in the whole crea- tion. I'll quit my country—do you hear that?—I'll quit my country!"

These words had an awful sound, and Allie, who had no time to reason, really felt that he was somehow to blame for the situation, in which he had only done what was right and proper.

" You make that dog drop that cane, and then you *hold* him by the neck until I get to, the street. Now you take hold of him, and don't you let him go until I'm clear out

of the way. Why, if I had such a dog as that I'd hang
him so high that he'd never come down. Sam Adams
ought to be prosecuted. But the crown will take care of
him. Now you hold the dog, and give me my cane."

Allie obeyed. He caught the dog by his neck, took
the cane from his mouth, and respectfully handed it to the
doctor. He felt safe in doing so with the dog in his grasp.

"I'd cane you now, you little Sam-Adams rebel, if it
weren't for that dog," said the doctor. "But I will do it
yet. You shall feel that cane yet, and when you do feel
it you will feel it. It will make you smart. I can hardly
keep my hands off of you! Hold on to the dog; don't
you let him off; I want you to hear what I tell you.
You insulted the dignity of my office when you refused
to tell me about the guns, and you stole my cane. Hold
on to the dog I say, while I talk with you for your good.
'Tis for your own good that I am giving you advice.
Hold on to the dog!

"Boy, this is a lawless town—hold on to the dog!—
where boys run away from corrections and steal before
one's very eyes. Hold on to the dog!—whatever you
do, hold on to the dog!"

"I've only done just what I thought was right," said
Allie, crying.

"You may well cry, boy. You ain't so much to blame
as others. These people are all so blinded that they cannot see. When people dare to resist the will of a king,

what can be expected of their children? You hold on to
the dog, and let me repeat to you what I have to say.
You see that cane? You see it, don't you?"

" Yes, sir."

" I'd raise it up, if it weren't for the dog. He's bitten
at two or three already. That dog is a rebel and a traitor. Sam Adams is in him. Well, as I said, you see that
cane?"

" Yes, sir."

" Well, you'll feel it some day, else I'll quit my
country."

The doctor stared at Allie so that he might feel the
awful import of the words "quit my country." What
would the world do then?

The doctor moved slowly away for a few paces.

" Now you hold on to that dog, and don't let him break
the peace, and I'll run. Hold on tight! "

Allie obeyed.

The doctor suddenly turned and trudged toward the
street. As he felt safe again he looked back, and raised
his cane and shook it so that Allie could see it, and
shouted:

" I'll be even with you yet. Ay, ay!"

Allie and Queue went down to the trees near the
marshes, where the Public Garden now is. Allie was
crying. The dog leaped up and down around him, as if
sympathizing with him and trying to comfort him.

The doctor would do all he could to injure him, but he could not see how he had acted wrong, or done anything that it was not right to do.

The sea-birds were winging their way over the marshes, and the wild geese in V-form honking in the high blue air. Spring was in the sky. The air was mild, and echoed distant sounds.

There was a boom of cannon at Cambridge. Was that one of the field-guns? The boy listened, and wondered at life. What did all these things mean?

Would he ever receive the doctor's caning? Boom! Another gun! Would it be Sam Adams or Dr. Oliver who would have to go? Boom! Boom!

CHAPTER XXI.

HERE was a soldier in the British camp in Boston whom we will call Merriweather, who had a keen sense of humor, and whose delight it was to go over to Cambridge to see the queer farmer-volunteers as they came into camp, and to study their dialect, which at that time was not unfrequently what has come to be called "Yankee." He gathered up the old phrases of the time, the queer provincial words, and used to repeat them, to the great amusement of the soldiers in camp.

Some of the Yankee volunteers at Cambridge did indeed present a very comical appearance, as, mustered in their farm clothes, they were summoned to parade. They, for the most part, had no military training, and did not understand military terms. To a trained British soldier, officered by courtly men, the parade of such soldiers was comical indeed.

Merriweather went to see the Yankee farmers parade as one would go to a fair. It has been privately said among the old people of Cambridge that Washington himself was

201

struck with the ludicrousness of the dress of the farmer regiments when he first took command of the army. But those men meant fight. Red coats and gold lace were no match for such a spirit.

One day as Allie, with his drum, was crossing the Common, he saw a large company of British soldiers laughing and singing under the trees.

He stopped to listen. The redcoats were singing his tune, "Yankee Doodle."

He drew nearer and listened again. He heard the men's voices ring out:

> " Yankee Doodle, Doodle doo,
> Yankee Doodle Dandy;
> Mind the music and the step,
> Yankee Doodle Dandy!"

It was Merriweather, who was entertaining the soldiers off duty under the cool trees.

He drew nearer. He knew Merriweather, who recognized him.

" Here, my fine lad," said Merriweather, " you play that tune for Sam Adams. You stole it. I have written some words for it. They are not Sam Adams's words. ' The Sam Adams Regiments' are not here now, as you will find. Lord Howe is not a Dalrymple nor a Governor Hutchinson. But you can drum!"

There arose a shout from the soldiers, "Give it to us again!"

" Fayreweather, there, you little rebel, you play in the chorus, and use your drum-sticks lively, now."

Merriweather rose up and began to read a very comical ballad that he had written, pronouncing certain words through his nose, in a manner that raised a great laugh. After every verse the men would sing the chorus.

Allie drummed at the first chorus, but after listening to the description of " Captain Washington upon his slapping stallion," he refused to play again.

" Play," shouted Merriweather, " play!"

Allie refused to obey.

The queer ballad was as follows, and was read by the comic poet in an odd way with interpolated dialogue :

> " Father and I went down to camp,
> Along with Captain Goodwin,
> Where we *see* the men and boys
> As thick as hasty-*puddin*'."

" *Sing!* "

The soldiers sang the chorus.

While they were singing old Dr. Oliver appeared, with cane and wig. He looked keenly at Allie, and said, " You haven't got your dog with you, have you? "

> " There was *Captain* Washington
> Upon a *slapping* stallion,
> A-giving orders to his men—
> I *guess* there was a million."

"*Sing!* Sing, Fayreweather. Roll your drum lively, now. There is great *doin's* over there to Cambridge!"

"Why don't you drum?" said Dr. Oliver to Allie.

> "And then the feathers on his hat,
>   They looked so *'tarnal fine-a*,
> I wanted *peckily* to get,
>   To give to my Jemima."

"Sing all!"

The chorus rang out merrily.

"Boy," said Dr. Oliver, "you remember that caning I have been promising you? Now you drum, or I will on you. You hear that?"

> "And then they had a *swampin'* gun,
>   As large as log of maple,
> On a *deuced* little cart—
>   A load for father's cattle."

"That must have been one of the guns that ran out of the town without legs or wheels. Sing!"

> "And every time they fired it off
>   It took a horn of powder;
> It made a noise like father's gun,
>   Only a *nation* louder."

"They say that the schoolboys stole the guns that were in the gun-house. How is that, Fayreweather? Sing!"

> "I went as near to it myself
>   As Jacob's *underpinnin'*,
> And father went *as near again*—
>   I thought the *deuce* was in him."

"Brave man, weren't he, Fayreweather?"

> "Cousin Simon grew so bold,
>   I thought he would have cocked it;
> It scared me so, I shrinkéd off,
>   And hung by father's pocket."

"Maybe that gun is one of those that went off in the air. The people hereabout seem to expect to see those guns again some day. Maybe they will, and Fayreweather here will drum."   ⦁

> "And Captain Davis had a gun,
>   He *kind-a* clapped his hand on't,
> And stuck a crooked stabbing-iron
>   Upon the little end on't."

"Boy, drum, I tell you!" said Dr. Oliver.
"I don't drum for these."
"These! Whom do you drum for?"
"I drum for Sam Adams."
The poet continued:

> "And there I *see* a pumpkin-shell
>   As big as mother's basin,
> And every time they touched it off
>   They scampered *like* the *nation*."

"You drum for Sam Adams, do you?" said Dr. Oliver, when the poet paused. "Let me only put my hand on you and I'll play such a tune on you that you will remember as long as you have any breath."

The poet continued:

> " And there I see a little keg,
> Its heads were made of leather;
> They knocked upon't with little sticks,
> To call the folks together."

" How would you like to go over *there* and drum, Fayre-weather?"

" I would like it well, sir."

" You would?"   And the poet went on:

> " And then they'd *fife away like fun*,
> And play on *cornstalk* fiddles;
> And some had *ribbons*, red as blood,
> All wound about their middles."

" They might ribbon you, Fayreweather.   How grand you would feel with your ribbons all on, if you could only come skipping down the Neck, drumming Washington into Boston!   Maybe you will some day."

> " The troopers, too, would gallop up
> And fire right in our faces;
> It scared me almost half to death
> To see them run such races!"

Dr. Oliver moved toward Allie slyly several times, but the boy sidled away.

The poet continued:

> " Old Uncle Sam *come* then to change
> Some pancakes and some onions
> For *'lasses cakes*, to carry home
> To give his wife and young ones."

The poet threw up his hands and drew down his face with a fearful grimace, as he said:

> "I *see* another *snarl* of men
> A-digging graves, they told me,
> So *'tarnal* long, so *'tarnal* deep,
> They 'tended they should hold me."

"That's the army that expects to drive Lord Howe out of Boston!"

> "It scared me so, I *hooked* it off,
> Nor slept, as I remember,
> Nor turned about till I got home,
> Locked up in mother's chamber."

"Sing all!"

He swung the ballad in the air, and the men sang the chorus over and over again.

At the end of the reading and singing a British officer laid his hand on Allie's shoulder.

"Now you shall drum."

"Or else scamper home to mother," said another.

But Allie refused. Dr. Oliver moved toward him.

"Here, give me your drum," said the officer.

Allie leaped away. He ran toward his home for a few steps, then he turned toward the marshes, leaped into a boat, and was paddling for Lechmere Point. Dr. Oliver and a soldier followed him.

"Where are you going?" shouted the soldier.

"To Cambridge!" cried Allie. "I drum for Sam Adams!"

"Come back!" shouted the doctor. "Come back, I say; come back!" The paddles moved forward.

"I'm coming back," said Allie.

"When?" shouted the doctor.

"When Washington comes!" answered Allie.

"I shan't be here then," said the doctor to the soldiers. "I'll quit my country!"

CHAPTER XXII.

THE NIGHT BEFORE THE GREAT SURPRISE.

ILL you give me a pass to the town through the lines?" asked Allie of an orderly of General Ward.

"Yes, if you will promise to return to headquarters at midnight and report all that you see and hear. You could be trusted, if any one. It will be a serious day in Boston to-morrow. The morning will bring doomsday to the town. The troops are already moving, but it is a still march; they will need no drummer. They may need one by daylight."

"I will be here," said Allie.

"Or arrested as a spy," said the orderly. "How will you pass the gates?"

"I will go by boat."

"What if you are challenged?"

"I am an unarmed boy; I would say to 'Who goes there?' 'A boy.' They would not stop a boy in a boat in the night."

"But why do you wish to go?"

"Great events are at hand. I wish to look into the old home window, and to see if the British camps are prepared for the night march."

"I will speak with the general," said the orderly.

"Tell him," said Allie, "that if the British should discover that the army is moving to Dorchester Heights, I will be the first to report it at headquarters. I am young, but I know Boston and the British camp."

The orderly went to the headquarters on Fort Hill, and held a consultation with the officers. He presently returned with a pass, and said, "You may go. As soon as the British discover the movement of the army, return and report to me. At any event, return before morning."

It was a still March night. The moon shone with a dim light, yet revealed ordinary objects in outline. Allie was soon through the lines, and he did not find it difficult to secure a boat, as he well knew the wharfages of the arm of the sea. He was not molested. The British army were off their guard, or thinking only of the cannonade which for several days had been going on from the hills on the opposite side of the town.

Allie landed and passed up Purchase Street. The house of Sam Adams was occupied by British troops. The men were at their cards, and a sentinel was pacing up and down the street.

"All is well!"

He stopped before his own home. The light was burning in the kitchen, a simple tallow dip, and against it he could discern the head of his mother.

He passed into the yard. The gate made a noise as he opened it, and he saw his mother's form move, start up, and heard her feet hurrying toward the door.

He stood under a tree at the foot of the back door-steps. His mother opened the door and listened. She heard the sentinel pacing to and fro.

" All is well!"

" Phillis, come here," said Mrs. Fayreweather. " I thought I heard a noise; the gate seemed to open, and I have a feeling as though some one were here. I have a sense as though Allie were here. I hope that nothing has happened to the boy."

Phillis came to the door. The heavens suddenly blazed, and a cannon thundered on the western hills. A slow cannonade was being kept up on the hills of the Charles and Mystic to divert the attention of the British officers.

" It is dangerous for us to be here," said Phillis. " We cannot tell what is going to happen."

A laugh of the officers in the Sam Adams house over their cards rang out on the air. Was it because some one had unexpectedly won, or over the report of the cannon?

It was still again. The sentinel passed by with his lantern.

" All is well!"

A gleam from the lantern swept through the yard.

15

" Mrs. Fayreweather," said Phillis, in a scared, faltering voice, " Mrs. Fayreweather!"

" What, Phillis? "

" I thought I saw something."

" Where, Phillis? "

" There! O Mrs. Fayreweather, look there! It is Allie. It is his apparition, or else a death-fetch. It is he."

Phillis was terribly frightened. She turned around and around, wringing her hands.

" It is his form, but not of this earth. O Mrs. Fayreweather, this is a dreadful night!"

The still air was again rent by the report of a cannon. A missile screamed in the sky.

Mrs. Fayreweather slowly went down the steps, peering into the dark.

" Don't go," said Phillis, " I'm afraid."

" Follow me," said Mrs. Fayreweather. " I see a form under the tree. "Allie, Allie Fayreweather, is that you? "

" Mother, don't speak aloud. I can't talk with you. Great events are at hand. Hide in cellar to-morrow," he whispered.

The sentinel's voice was heard :

" All is well!"

" Mother, all is well. Good-by."

" Yes, my boy, all is well. But what brought you here? "

"I have secret orders; but you brought me here. I wanted to see you through the window-pane. You must not speak of this. Tell Phillis that."

"Allie, let me kiss you."

The boy held his mother in his arms.

She only said, "Philip!" and added, "I think all the time of him."

The hills thundered again. The heavens blazed. Allie whispered to his mother:

"They are doing that to protect the movement of the army. To-morrow will be an awful day for the British in Boston. Mother, rise early and listen, and you will hear me drum."

He broke away from her and went to the British camps. He was a boy, and was not challenged.

Everywhere sentinels were pacing to and fro, and saying, "All is well!"

The soldiers were talking of the slow cannonade from the river hills. The officers were expecting that an attempt might be made to destroy the town from those quarters, and a grand movement was about to be made to dislodge and silence the batteries there, as had been done at Bunker Hill.

None seemed to dream that a silent army was then marching over a road of hay, and that in the morning guns would thunder almost over their heads.

Allie crept back to his boat. As he passed along to

the dark water toward the Roxbury end of the Neck, he heard the clocks striking twelve.

The Roxbury roads were silent. There were no lights to be seen anywhere. Yet the darkness was all alive with the passing of armed men and loads of arms. In Boston the sentinels were saying, " All is well!"

As he was about to enter the boat the silence was broken. He saw a light moving along the Neck Road, and heard the noise of wheels.

He stopped, for it occurred to him that the driver might be a messenger. He left the wharves, and glided quietly toward the highway.

The carriage was a gig, with a doctor's light in front. He knew that gig.

" Dr. Oliver's," he said. " He has been to see a patient on the Neck."

So it was. The doctor was riding home after making a call on some sick person, to whose bedside he had been summoned in the night. He had been near the moving army. Had he discovered the movement?

No. He was riding too easily to have made such a discovery.

As the gig came up the side-light flashed full in Allie's face.

The doctor started.

" You, Fayreweather boy ! I thought you were drumming at Cambridge. What brings you here at this time of night? If the guards get hold of you, my boy, you will not want for a lodging. You drum for Sam Adams?"

"Yes, for Adams and the new flag that has been raised for liberty—for the thirteen stripes!"

"I'd like to leave on you thirteen stripes, you little rebel. I wonder if I ever will?"

He took up his cane, that lay on his saddle-bags under the boot of the gig. He raised it and shook it, and seemed to be about to throw it.

"Don't throw away your cane, doctor. You will need it very soon; you will have to travel fast."

"Boy, what do you mean by that?"

"I don't think, doctor, that you will ever apply that cane to my back. The British in Boston must soon leave the town. They will find themselves surrounded, and a town cannot feed on the sea!"

"Then I'll have to quit my country. Sam Adams or I will have to go. That's so and also. Go 'long!" He spoke to the horse.

The gig rattled down the road. Allie saw the light on it zigzag away. It was the last time that he ever saw poor Dr. Oliver.

While the sentinels were saying, "All is well!" in Boston town, siege-cannon were being planted on the firm base of Dorchester Heights near those historic fields where the storm-tossed passengers of the "Mary and John" had made their first thanksgiving.

The lights gleamed on the hills to the west, where in the camps were the four field-pieces. The sentinels there paced to and fro and said, "All is well!"

Allie went safely back to the headquarters on the Roxbury Hill.

"Have they discovered anything?" asked the orderly.

"Nothing, sir."

"Then go to the Heights. They will need a drummer in the morning."

After Washington took command of the army under the great elm on Cambridge Common, the camps along the Charles grew, and the hills that encircled the town of Boston over the arms of the two rivers began to assume the appearance of fortresses. General Lee made his headquarters at Hobgoblin Hall, which house and old slave quarters may still be seen. Here he lived with his famous dog Spada, in a style which he thought befitted his ambition. The other leading generals made headquarters of the fine old colonial places on the Mystic and the Charles.

The visitor to Boston should go to Prospect Hill if he would see the city and the harbor, and trace the circle of high camps in Washington's day. Boston looks like a Venice from this beautiful height.

Soon all of the hills to the south had become fortifications. The army was provided with siege-guns from Crown Point. Winter found the town under the fire of these high batteries. It only remained for Washington to cross the Neck and to surprise Dorchester Heights to bring a semicircle of guns to bear upon the town. This great surprise was now at hand.

The visitor should survey these historic fields from Dorchester Heights. Close at hand is the Castle (Fort Independence). In full view are the Milton Hills, where Governor Hutchinson lived, and a part of whose estate is yet to be seen. Beyond lies Quincy, the town of two Presidents, whose homes yet stand, and the green hill from whose top the wife of John Adams and her little son, John Quincy Adams, are said to have watched the battle of Bunker Hill in the long June afternoon. Beautiful are the scenes and traditions of all these hills, and nearly every one of them has on its summit parks with cool trees, fountains, and historic records. My reader will love to visit them all.

The ways between the hills are also historic. As the visitor goes out to Roxbury by Washington Street, he may stop to visit the house where General Warren lived, and read its stone records. He may turn aside and go to Shirley Street, near the Dudley Street stables, and find the ruin of the grand mansion of Governor Shirley, in what was once the Roxbury Fields. And at the Falls of Milton, or Milton Lower Mills, one should tarry long, for close at hand is the old house, with an historical inscription, in which the famous " Suffolk Resolves " were passed, declaring that the acts of Parliament in regard to the colonies were no longer to be obeyed.

Think of the tremendous events in history for which all these humble places, as they appear now, stand: the fall of Louisburg and of the French empire in America, with the ruin of the once fine mansion on Shirley Street, overlooking the ancient sea-meadows; the fall of the British power in America with the house at the Lower Mills; and the rise of America with the colonial houses of Quincy. Such scenes as these are worth a pilgrimage. In these places the liberties of the world were born.

CHAPTER XXIII.

 CRY rang through the streets of Boston in the morning, a wild cry—" The Heights! the Heights!"

A gun thundered over the town. Lord Howe turned his eyes toward Dorchester Heights in amazement.

" The provincials," he said, " have done more in a single night than my army in months!"

He stared into the air. The Heights glowed in the sunrise.

The redoubt on the Heights held the town at its mercy. The British officers at the Province House saw that they must leave by the sea.

There was heard in the distance the rattle of a drum. It was playing the tune of the British when " The Sam Adams Regiments " landed at the Castle. Mrs. Fayreweather heard it, and she knew the notes. Dr. Oliver heard it, and said, " Now I *shall* have to quit my country, *also!* "

219

The morning of the 5th of March, the day which re-called the Boston Massacre, brought a happy day to Allie. With his drum he led the march up Dorchester Heights, to the very spot where he had first heard the Yankee Doodle tune, when "The Sam Adams Regiments" were embarking.

The scene was thrilling. On the crown of the hill that morning sat Washington on his horse—the "strapping stallion" of which Allie had first heard in the queer ballad whose chorus had been so lustily sung by the British soldiers on the Common.

Washington from his station looked down upon the town, the Castle, and the harbor. On the hills he saw the preparations of his own army for battle; below him, the preparations of the British. He was sure that the town was in his power. He was right. Lord Howe himself saw that the army of the crown must disembark.

How strange it was! A few days before, Washington had been made the subject of a comedy in the British theatre in Boston. The play was called "The Siege of Boston." While the audience were yet laughing at a comical figure on the stage which burlesqued Washington, there came a sudden call to arms, which the audience first thought was a part of the play.

After an ineffectual attempt to attack the army on the Heights from the sea, Lord Howe prepared to surrender the town, and to disembark with his troops under the cover of the Castle. Thus was the first contest of the Revolution won. The end would be Yorktown.

There were merry notes in Allie's drum. The boy longed to play again in the streets of the town.

He would not have to wait long. The grand march was at hand!

CHAPTER XXIV.

ALLIE'S DRUM LEADS THE TRIUMPHAL MARCH.

T was the 20th of March, 1776. The people of Boston had been apprised that on that day General Washington would enter the town in triumph. He would ride down from the hills by way of the Neck, followed by the army. The bell-ringers were ready to receive him. The balconies were cleared for outlooks. The people from the country flocked in over the ferries and down the Neck.

The morning came with exultant gatherings and pealings of bells. The army was put in gala array. The people surged out toward the Neck to meet it.

It came at last, the drum corps and fifers leading the way. What was the tune they were playing? It was the same tune that "The Sam Adams Regiments" had played on landing at the Castle.

And who was leading the drummers in this merry tune? It as a manly young man, so late a boy—Allie Fayreweather.

A part of the army came past the house where the Suffolk Resolves were passed, now to be seen at the foot of Milton Hill close to the Falls and the depot. The Resolves were to the effect that the acts of the British Parliament in regard to America were not to be heeded. Another portion of the army passed near the house of Governor Shirley, in Roxbury, the once hero of the conquest of Louisburg. As the troops united from various points they came to the place of the old Liberty Tree, where the Sons of the Revolution had been wont to meet, which the British had reduced to fourteen cords of wood.

And now, following the drum, with Washington on a noble steed, the bells all ringing and the people all shouting for joy, the guard procession reached the West Schoolhouse.

Queue had run up the Neck to meet Allie, and he followed him, now and then leaping up by his side.

As the head of the procession reached the schoolhouse the patriot schoolmaster appeared at the door. Dr. Story joined him. A group had gathered in the yard. Old Surry was there, and Phillis. Blingo was also there.

Hark! What was that? A gun thundered from the hills. It was one of the four cannon. Perhaps the one called to-day the " Hancock."

Hark! What was that? Another gun! It shook the town. That, too, was one of the four guns. It may have been the one now called the "Adams."

As Washington passed the West Schoolhouse he lifted

his hat.   Poor Old Surry bowed over almost to the
ground.

The town was shaken by the cannon again.   The patriot
schoolmaster covered his face.   The bells clanged, and the
people wept while they shouted.

The Province House stood deserted.   The Old South
Church had been used as a riding-school, and was inwardly
a ruin.   There Warren had entered the room by the window, in the black robes of an orator, and delivered his
great oration.   There a man or a boy, as the legend runs,
had been appointed to throw an egg at him, when he
should speak against the king, as a signal for the arrest
of Adams, Hancock, and all the patriots.   The egg was
broken in the crowd.   What might have been the destiny
of America had that egg been thrown?

The Town House was the town's now, so also was
Faneuil Hall.   The people thronged the steps of these
buildings on this glorious day.   The Hancock House had
been used as his headquarters by Lord Percy.   The latter
was now tossing on the sea, near the Castle.

But the home of Adams—how had that fared during the siege?   The home of him who had organized the
Revolution, seconded the motion for making the same
George Washington commander-in-chief of the American
armies, and who was now urging forward at Philadelphia
the proclamation of the Declaration of Independence, on
the ground of political necessity!

We will let Mr. Adams's greatest biographer give the picture:

"Boston had lately been evacuated by the British troops. Samuel Adams, in his letters to his friends in Massachusetts, warns them against the possibility of the return of the enemy in the summer, and urges a defence of the whole New England seacoast. It was with anxious interest that he learned the particulars of the events and the condition of his family. During the tedious months that the siege of Boston had continued, his residence in Purchase Street was occupied by royal officers, who had wantonly mutilated the interior, destroyed the outhouses, and, with spiteful hatred of the proprietor, had cut into the window-panes obscene and blasphemous writings, some of them ridiculing his religious habits. Caricatures were placed upon the walls, and the garden was completely ruined. On entering the house after the departure of its late occupants a firebrand was found on the floor, perhaps fallen there from the fireplace accidentally, as no intention is known to have been entertained by the enemy of burning the town. The family returned, with the design of occupying the house, soon after the departure of the British, but they found the premises uninhabitable. Many windows were broken out, doors unhinged and burned for fuel, and every species of wanton destruction were visible. Mr. Adams was never pecuniarily able thereafter to repair the ravages of these vandals, and the family went to live in Dedham, where they resided until 1778."

Phillis Wheatley followed the gay procession. She tried again and again to bring her sharp face and high forehead before Washington's eye. Would he recognize her now in his day of glory, when the cannon were booming on the hills and the bells ringing in the steeples?

At one point of the processional march the general and his officers swept aside and bowed to a singing and shouting concourse of people. Phillis was among them. The officers gave her a welcome.

" He saw me," said the poor girl, "and gave me a glance which will make me happy while I live!" She covered her face and turned toward the wall and cried.

The Widow Fayreweather was there, with the haunting thought of her dead boy, whose body would now be brought back from Bunker Hill to be buried in the Granary Burying-ground. Annie was there.

" Master Holbrooke," she said, " were those guns which were fired the same as the ones hidden here ? "

" You know the secret, then," said the master. " They are either the same ones, or else those have already gone forward to New York to compel the British to evacuate the country."

" That was a great hour when you put your lame foot on that wood-box, Master Holbrooke!"

" A great hour, madam. Events make it so."

The army halted on the Common near the schoolhouse. The greening sward was soon covered with weary men.

Allie crossed the street with his drum, and his brother Andrew followed him.

The two met their mother and Andrew's bride.

"You are thinking of Philip," said Andrew.

"Yes," said Mrs. Fayreweather. "Of whom else could I be thinking?"

"Mother," said Allie, "I have something I want to say; it will not let me rest. Andrew, I want you to hear it. Annie, I want you to hear it."

"What is it, my son?" cried the widow.

"Philip drew a white kernel of corn in the schoolhouse, but he changed it when he clasped Andrew's hand. *He left the white kernel in Andrew's hand, and withdrew Andrew's red kernel into his own.* I saw him."

There followed a silence. Each saw in those words the picture of a noble soul.

The tears streamed down the eyes of the mother and her sons on that March day.

"I am glad that I have such sons," said the widow. "It is of such men as that that our army is composed. The cause will succeed. Philip is dead, but what were death to dishonor! This is a glorious day!"

Then followed another eventful day. It was the 27th of March, 1776. Although Boston was evacuated on the 17th, the fleet still lingered below the Castle. On board

16

the transports were a thousand Tories, many of them among the most prosperous and learned people of the colony. Among them was Dr. Oliver, who was now indeed "going to quit his country," but he looked back with sorrow.

Allie went out to Dorchester Heights again where he had first heard the new tune. The sky was clear with the warm blue of spring, and the waters stretched away foam-flecked but calm. The fleet lay in the sun, the long line of ships crossing the inner harbor and pointing toward the sea.

There was a whitening of sail on all the vessels, a flutter of flags, and more than a thousand exiles crowded the decks, and looked back to the three-hilled town, and thought of their homes, and the old days of happiness and promise.

The fleet was moving. Slowly the ships left the inner harbor and passed from sight into the bay. The four guns had led the way to events that had compelled the evacuation of the town; would they also lead the way to larger fields, and compel the surrender of the British army in America? Would they fulfil Sam Adams's dream?

As nightfall came the last transport of the British fleet faded from view. The sea was empty, and the town was awed and still. Allie marched down the Neck, saying to all he met, "The fleet is gone!"

He passed the ruin of the Liberty Tree, and came to

the West Schoolhouse. The patriot schoolmaster was
alone there with his copybooks. Allie rolled his drum
to the merry tune, and entered the house.

"That was a great day, master, when you had the guns
in the wood-box. The fleet is gone!" •

The master rose. He thought of seven stormy years.

"And where, Allie, are the patriot scholars?"

"Gone, or going!"

The master looked out on the Common. All was preparation there for the departure of troops for the greater
struggle for liberty, to which the evacuation of Boston was
the trumpet-call to victory.

Sam Adams had said on the Woburn Hills, on hearing
the guns at Lexington, "What a glorious morn is this!"

The two sat down on the wood-box. Old Surry appeared at the door, and Queue. One after another of the
townsmen came in, each one saying, "The fleet is gone!"

There was a peal of bells. They rang over a delivered
town, and the Boston bells at that time were the voice of
the people, ringing out their joy and tolling their woe.

The schoolroom filled with people.

"What a glorious night is this!" said the patriot schoolmaster.

The people felt his words, and at last followed Allie's
drum into the street, saying, "What a glorious night is
this!"

The cause of liberty was advancing to new fields, but its

first battle was won; and ever worthy to be remembered is the school which defended the guns, and its patriot schoolmaster.

*   *   *   *   *

Years passed.

There used to walk down the malls of Boston Common an old man seventy-five years of age.   He had made Presidents of the United States by his influence, but he was not, never had been, or would be, President.   He was the governor of Massachusetts.

As he passed by West Street and out of the Common to School Street the children followed him.   He was known and loved in all the schools, and the children used to follow the kindly and gracious old man wherever he went in his daily walks.

It was Sam Adams.

Look into the Granary Burying-ground as you pass. He sleeps there.

Boys, that man stood alone with faith in American independence in his heart for nearly twenty years.   His life is a lesson.   Have faith in your purpose.   Time will be your friend.   Be willing to stand alone for the right!

CHAPTER XXV.

ET the visitor to Boston go to Bunker Hill Monument, which stands in the centre of the old redoubt on what was then known as Breed's Hill. Let him ascend the spiral flight of stone steps, two hundred and ninety-five in number. Let him rest on his way in the cool echoing air, and look out of the apertures in the stone as he ascends. At the top, in a chamber seventeen feet high, he will find the two brass field-pieces.

These were hurried from the siege of Boston, flushed with victory, to New York. They did service on nearly all the great fields of the war; they were the voice of Massachusetts in the long contest. When the war was over, the State wished them to stand as a monument to her honor. Congress gave them back to the State, and the State gave them to the monument. They were for many years the glory of Boston's most historic military company, the Ancient and Honorable Artillery.

Let him look out of the four open windows with iron shutters, to the north, south, east, and west. He may then

trace all of the places associated with our story: the Common, the Old S uth Church, the Old North Church, Copp's
Hill, the Charles and the Mystic rivers, the circle of hills,
Charlestown, Cambridge, the harbor, and Fort Independence, which was the Castle.

On the walls he may read the inscription on the two
brass cannon, and kindly recall the wood-box in the West
Schoolhouse and the heroic patriot schoolmaster:

SACRED TO LIBERTY.

THIS IS ONE OF THE FOUR CANNON WHICH CONSTITUTED THE

WHOLE TRAIN OF FIELD ARTILLERY POSSESSED BY THE

BRITISH COLONIES OF

NORTH AMERICA,

AT THE COMMENCEMENT OF THE

WAR,

ON THE 19TH OF APRIL, 1775.

THIS CANNON AND ITS FELLOW, BELONGING TO A

NUMBER OF CITIZENS OF

BOSTON,

WERE USED IN MANY ENGAGEMENTS

DURING THE WAR.

THE OTHER TWO, THE PROPERTY OF THE GOVERNMENT OF

MASSACHUSETTS, WERE TAKEN BY THE ENEMY.

———

BY ORDER OF THE UNITED STATES,

IN CONGRESS ASSEMBLED

MAY 19TH, 1788.

Let him close his eyes, and he m.. see in his fancy Sam Adams walking the streets of Boston town alone, but with the dream of American independence in his mind. Then let him go away, and live for his own best self, as did this patriot whom Liberty will ever crown!

THE END.